A 'HOW TO MAKE A MONSTER' NOVELLA

BY FELIX I.D. DIMARO

Daily SPECIAL

Written by FELIX I.D. DIMARO
Originally published in the collection of nightmares,
How To Make A Monster: The Loveliest Shade of Red

Cover Artwork: Rosco Nischler
Interior Artwork: Rosco Nischler, Katrina Canedo
Typography: Courtney Swank
Editing: Ally Sztrimbely

Copyright ©2023 by FELIX I.D. DIMARO

This is a work of fiction. Names, characters, businesses, places, events and incidents are either the products of the author's imagination or used in a fictitious manner. Any resemblance to actual persons, living or dead, or actual events is purely coincidental.

ALSO BY FELIX I.D. DIMARO

How To Make A Monster: The Loveliest Shade of Red

Bug Spray: A Tale of Madness

Viral Lives: A Ghost Story

2222

The Fire On Memory Lane

The Corruption of Philip Toles

Black Bloom: A Story of Survival

Us In Pieces: Stories of Shattered Souls

Humane Sacrifice: The Story of the Aztec Killer

Warning

This story contains mature content, including profane language, adult themes, and scenes depicting graphic violence and explicit sex.

Discretion is advised.

The scariest monsters are human beings and what we will do to each other.

Jared Harris

Daily SPECIAL

- DISCOUNT BRAND FROZEN DINNER..........................01
- PAN FRIED SPAM AND RAMEN NOODLES.................02
- CROCODILIAN..03
- BREASTS...04
- MEDIOCRE STEW...05
- BLACK BIRD FEATHERS...06
- CALF'S BRAINS AND COW TONGUE.........................07
- OUROBOROS..08
- LOBSTER BISQUE..09
- MACARONI BATHED IN CHEESE................................10
- STUFFED PORTOBELLO MUSHROOMS.......................11
- LASAGNA..12
- PORK CHOPS..13
- CROW'S FEET...14
- A DISH BEST SERVED COLD.......................................15
- TAMALES...16
- CHEESECAKE...17
- A BUFFET OF FLESH...18
- TOMATO SOUP..19

DISCOUNT BRAND FROZEN DINNER.................O1

Hubert Jenkins was an addict, a junkie, a man of continuous craving. Not for drugs or booze, he partook of those vices only on rare occasions. Ever since he was a child, Hubert Jenkins, or Chef Hue as he would eventually be called, had been addicted to the idea of fame.

    As a child, before becoming obsessed with the notion of being a celebrity chef, Hubert had desperately wanted to be a professional wrestler. That was until he broke his collarbone while being choke-slammed on the grass of his elementary school yard by a much bigger classmate (who, incidentally, did go on to become a professional wrestler). While his mother, a large and loud woman, wailed over his hospital bed, threatening to sue each teacher, the principal, and even the janitor at his elementary school, Hubert, a pudgy and awkward child, quickly eliminated any idea of athletics from his future as he ruminated over his broken bone. He decided that his low tolerance for pain (and for his mother's hysterics) outweighed his obsession with wrestling. Instead, he decided he wanted to be an actor.

Hubert's terrible lack of stage presence and coordination put an end to that dream the day he tripped over his own feet and tumbled off the stage while playing the role of Malvolio in William Shakespeare's *Twelfth Night* during a ninth-grade drama class performance for the entire school. Needless to say, high school did not go very well for Hubert. Falling off the stage had fractured the same collarbone he had broken during his grade school misadventures as an aspiring professional wrestler. And though the bone would heal, and the bruises would fade, the kids would never allow him to forget his mishap, referring to him from that point forward with such poetic epithets as: Twelfth Flight, Shakesqueer, and Mal-bone-io. As a result, Hubert's four-year high school tour was full of insults and beatings while being bereft of anything even remotely close to sex. Like Malvolio, there was never a man so notoriously abused.

Still awkward and pudgy into his teenage years, Hubert quickly realized that what he was best at was eating. Hubert loved food. He admittedly ate too much of it, but he never let that, or anything else, stop him from his indulgences. Though his mother did nothing to get in the way of his gluttony, her idea of preparing a meal was heating a discount brand frozen dinner in the microwave and plopping it on a TV tray in front of her son. He ate the meals she placed in front of him readily enough; ate seconds and thirds in fact. He would always accept more, but what he truly wanted was *better*.

What Hubert Jenkins craved was something special. His mother, Lenora Jenkins (or Lenny as she liked to be called), much like her bounty of frozen foods, was plentiful – by girth, by mass, by sheer volume – but she had never become better. Lenny Jenkins ate a ton, but was a lousy cook, and was far too broke to afford any of the delicacies Hubert so badly yearned for. Hubert's father had left them both when the boy was just six years old. Hubert, while growing up, had wondered at times if his father had left because of his mother's awful cooking.

Not wanting to have to rely on anyone to get his food fix, and definitely not wanting to end up like his lonely, poor, doting, useless-in-the-kitchen-yet-still-incredibly-overweight mother, Hubert decided he needed to learn how to cook. At the age of fourteen, Hubert began to teach himself, reading any cookbook he could get his hands on, watching whichever cooking program he could whenever his mother went to bed (or, more accurately, when she passed out drunk on their couch, leaving the remote control to him). He would steal a few sips of courage from the not-quite-empty bottles and cans of booze Lenny left all over the house, and, while she slept, he would cook.

The boy taught himself the culinary arts. Young Hubert often spent the savings from his two-dollar-a-week allowance at the nearby grocery store buying whichever ingredients were on sale or discounted because they were about to go rotten. He never once considered asking his mother to help him with the food items, understanding that if she knew what he was up to, she would try to stop it. He hated her for that. For never wanting anything more than what already was. Never wanting either of them to be better.

For every time his knife betrayed him and opened his flesh, and for every time he seared his skin, he became more and more incensed by his mother. She should have been the one to show him how to handle the knife and its cutting board; she should have been the one to show him which pot was best used to prepare which dish, but she wasn't that person. He resented her for that.

He would often stand over her prone, passed out body, smiling darkly while chewing contentedly on whichever recipe he had dared to bring to life during her slumber. On one particular night, he knelt beside her as his mouth was still working on a bite of the scratch-made hamburger that the television had told him was crucial to make. Lenny always wore a shawl in the house, and she usually kept a bottle of something hot beneath it, cradled between her torso and arm. On this night, he plucked that bottle from underneath one of her flabby arms, brought it to his lips and drew from it as though it were life-redeeming water. The liquid burned him from the tip of his tongue to his throat before it turned into a pleasurable warmth amidst his sternum. He equated that pleasurable warmth with certainty.

Hubert had looked down at his prone mother, noticing the bulge of her belly, the girth of her jowl. He saw how the material of her yoga pants (which she had never for even an instant worn for anything other than comfort) strained against the heft of her gigantic thighs and calves. He witnessed her becoming more. He knew he wanted better.

The young Hubert Jenkins sipped from the bottle of whiskey, grinned at his unconscious mother, and decided that he wouldn't be under her control for much longer.

PAN FRIED SPAM AND RAMEN NOODLES.........02

It shouldn't come as a complete surprise that Hubert didn't have many friends. His high school experience and narrow focus on fame had made it difficult for him to obtain and maintain close personal connections. Not that he minded one way or the other. His mindset was such that he believed fame would eventually be his best friend, and with that best friend would come many, many others. It was just a matter of time until Hubert Jenkins would become the most famous person out of Milan, Ohio since Thomas Edison. He had no doubt of that. The thought of that fame gave him the same thrills that the other kids his age obtained from the kissing and heavy petting that went on beneath the steps and in the shadowy corners of his high school.

    At sixteen years old, Hubert got a job at a restaurant just outside of town in the neighboring city of Telesto, Ohio. Although he was just a dishwasher, he took careful note of everything the cooks and chefs did, quietly honing his skills. The job didn't pay much, but it paid enough for him to put aside money for culinary school. He also stole from the restaurant fridge whenever he could in order to save money on groceries and obtain the things his mother refused (or couldn't afford) to buy.

Lenora Jenkins ate herself to death when Hubert was eighteen years old. No one, least of all Hubert, was shocked to hear that she had died of a heart attack even though she was only forty-two.

When Hubert had stopped cooking in secret and began encouraging Lenny to eat his healthy meals, she had doggedly refused, opting instead for some of her favorites: peanut butter and butter sandwiches, frozen microwave meals, and the dozen or so stale donuts she received each day at the end of her shift at the coffee shop at the end of their street. Also included among her favorite things to consume were her cigarettes and her whisky (she drank the golden-brown liquid more often than she drank water).

It took Hubert a few years to understand that his mother had refused to eat his meals because she had not wanted to encourage his ambitions. Lenny had not wanted him to achieve his goals because, if he did, he would have inevitably left her behind. When she had first discovered that he'd been cooking "that shit" behind her back (which was the way she had always put it), she became irate, throwing out an entire pan of scalloped potatoes. The next time it had been a pot of chicken noodle soup poured down the drain. The time after that it was a homemade pizza, much of which had wound up on the neighbor's roof after she had carried it to the backyard and treated it like a discus.

After a few more of these outrages, Hubert threatened to leave entirely if his mother didn't let him do what he thought was his calling. She had reluctantly relented but would never even so much as taste anything that Hubert created in their kitchen. In fact, the more his cooking improved, the more junk Lenny had eaten. He became better, she had continued to expand into more.

Her death came on a day that was a truly joyous one for Hubert. It was the day that he won a cooking competition which had pitted him against four other high school wannabe chefs. It was a smaller scale version of a competition he had seen on the Food Network for years, held by a popular food blog based in Telesto. Though he knew he wasn't an Iron Chef... yet, with this victory, he believed he was well on his way. The prize was five-hundred dollars and all the leftovers made by the competitors.

Afterward, Hubert ran into the little bungalow he and his mother called home. He cried out for her, proclaiming that he had won, that he was going to be something great. He told her that all the practice she had been putting up with was finally starting to pay off.

"You may not like it mama, but I'm gonna be a celebrity chef some day!" he had exclaimed while storming through the door on that windy day in August. He had mindlessly dropped the bags of food he'd been awarded, and only managed to remove one shoe before his excitement led him screaming into the house, yelling the details of his triumph at his mother.

Lenny was always home. Always responsive when Hubert returned from school or work, no matter how drunk or high she was. By that time, she had stopped working at the coffee shop and had been granted long-term disability based upon some health concern that was really just a by-product of her morbid obesity. Hubert heard no response to his ravings of victory on this occasion, though he didn't give that much thought. He was too excited, too elated. For the first time in as long as he could remember, he was full of genuine hope, ebullient with the idea that he perhaps did have what it took to be a top chef. He didn't want to celebrate with his mother so much as he wanted to rub it in her fat, unsupportive face.

In his excitement (and because he was off balance due to still having on the one shoe) Hubert lost his footing and went sprawling onto the hallway floor, landing flat on his stomach and making an **Ooomf** sound as the air was pushed out of him. Even that bit of embarrassment didn't dampen his mood or lesson his excitement. He still smiled as he struggled to catch his breath.

When he got to his feet, he removed the other shoe and forced himself to walk calmly rather than run the last few paces to the living room (which was just as much his mother's bedroom considering how often she passed out drunk there). And that is where he found her, as she usually was, on the couch in front of the television. It was blaring an episode of *Survivor*, the irony of which would become obvious to him within minutes. His mother's TV dinner tray was propped up in front of her, just as it usually was. But not much else was usual about this scene.

Lenora "Lenny" Jenkins was face down in a bowl of what Hubert would later learn was pan fried spam and ramen noodles. A still smoldering cigarette lay on top of a graveyard of butts within a generously sized ashtray near her head. She looked, to Hubert, like a pig at a trough. Her peach-colored shawl and fluffy pink house slippers only added to the imagery. Hubert had to chuckle at that. Later, he would think of all the wonderful leftovers in the fridge that he had made as he'd been practicing for the cooking competition.

There had been turkey pot pie, three cheese lasagna, baked herb and lemon tilapia, pan-seared flank steak, mashed potatoes rich with green onions and chives and cilantro and heavy on the butter, just the way his mother ordered it whenever they could afford to go to a restaurant. All of these things his mother could have eaten, all of these things Hubert had offered her, but in the end, she had decided to fry a tin of spam and a couple of dollar store packages of ramen. It was one final slight from his mother to him. Whenever he looked back on this day, he was always more upset about her choice of a final meal than he was about the fact that she was dead.

The floor around her had been littered with beer cans and her usual bottle of whiskey. She looked as though she had been enjoying the meal so much she had decided to forego cutlery altogether. Good enough to die for, he thought after he had tiptoed around her mess and pressed his fingers into the folds of flesh she called a neck in order to check for a pulse he already knew he would never find. The smell of shit and piss that filled the room was a pretty good indicator of her death.

During all of this, Hubert wondered how he would be able to afford a new sofa, soiled as theirs now was. He looked away from his mother's corpse, picked up the bottle of whiskey, took a swig, took another, and grimaced when it warmed his chest as it had the first time he had pilfered a swallow from her. A drink was appropriate for a day worthy of celebration. He wasn't going to let something like his mother keeling over put a damper on such a joyous occasion.

After putting down the bottle, Hubert had lowered the volume on the television, pulled out his cell phone, called for the death cab.

CROCODILIAN..**03**

While his mother may not have been a survivor, Hubert always had been. Sure, she had always been there physically, but she had never truly been there in a way that a boy needs his mama to be. For years, he had fended for himself while she was wasted and useless. Despite his own numerous flaws, Hubert had always been a cunning and ambitious young man. His long-term dream was to become a culinary celebrity, his immediate goal was culinary school.

   A week after finding his mother's corpse, he went to the organizers of the cooking competition he had won the day of Lenora's death. He poured his pudgy heart out, telling them that all he had ever wanted was to become a chef to make his mother proud. He wept tears of a crocodilian nature as he explained to them that he no longer had any family, and, because he had been so focused on his goals, he had never made many friends. He begged for them to help pay for his schooling. A scholarship of sorts. He went as far as to say he would give back his five-hundred-dollar prize money in exchange for the chance to live his dream and make his mother proud as she looked down on him from Heaven. Perhaps he should have been asking for a dramatic arts scholarship rather than one for food services, because his performance won them over.

The kids who had called him Mal-bone-io in school would have been swallowing their words had they seen him on that day.

In the end, he not only received quadruple the prize money originally awarded him, Hubert was also given the scholarship he had so longed for. And that is how the *Chop, Cook, Create Culinary Blog and Review* established *The Lenora Jenkins Memorial Scholarship for the Culinary Arts*. And how Hubert Jenkins became its first recipient.

Hubert didn't bother visiting his mother's grave before he left town for culinary school.

BREASTS..04

If his mother had tried Hubert's meals, she likely wouldn't have been as impressed as Hubert had once believed she would be. He received mediocre marks at Frederick Brown College in Telesto, one of the few schools in the state with a Culinary Arts program that had even considered his application on such short notice.

It had originally been his plan to work full time after high school until he could afford to pay his way through college.

Then he won the contest.
Then his mom died.
Then he saw his opportunity.
Then his plans had been expedited.

Perhaps that time between high school and college would have been beneficial to the honing of his craft. Instead, he barely managed to graduate from the Culinary Arts program at Frederick Brown, but graduate he did. Likely due more to his cunning than his cookery.

Thirteen years after completing the two-year Culinary Arts program, having had many jobs as a sous chef or line cook, and obtaining several large loans from a variety of financial institutions, Hubert was finally able to open his own restaurant, egotistically named *A Lovely Hue Restaurant and Bar*. He received equally mediocre reviews from those who dined at his establishment as he had from his college instructors. Despite the mediocrity, Hubert's restaurant was moderately successful.

Now, two years after the grand opening, if Hubert (who, at this point, was officially known as Chef Hue) had taken a step back and looked at his life, he would have understood that he was a pretty successful guy. He had accomplished a lifelong goal of owning his own restaurant, and he'd managed to open it in downtown Cincinnati, Ohio, after having grown up in one of the more rural towns in the state. Eventually, he made enough money to purchase his own condo just a few blocks from his restaurant and, even though he didn't really need to drive, he leased a brand-new honey-colored BMW M4 Coupé. He had even managed to lose seventy pounds soon after graduating from Frederick Brown, when all indications had pointed to an adulthood of obesity.

With the fancy car, the ritzy condo in the downtown core, the trimmer body, and the title of Head Chef, Chef Hue was able to get as many women as he wanted. And he wanted many women.

No one would ever call him Shakesqueer again.

The restaurant maintained steady business mainly due to its low prices and great ambiance. It was a hotspot for the college kids who just wanted cheap drinks, something edible to fill their bellies, and an affordable place to take their dates. Chef Hue was smart enough to have a hard-working team of promoters boost the restaurant's image relentlessly on the internet, resulting in a decent number of patrons on Friday and Saturday nights, and giving him just enough customers throughout the week to not have to worry about making rent or paying his staff. The moderate success was mainly from false reviews on various foody websites. Chef Hue had realized a funny thing about people: if they read enough positive reviews about pretty much anything, they could convince themselves to enjoy it whether it was truly a good product or not.

Chef Hue's promotion team (which primarily consisted of two young women who each considered herself his girlfriend – one was eighteen, the other twenty-two, and neither knew of the other's existence) would spend time finding every restaurant review site they could, and make sure to let the readers know just how amazing the food and service at *A Lovely Hue* was. Although the food was average at best, and the service was no better, the reviews seemed to keep customers coming in. Fake reviews. They were Chef Hue's bread and butter. It also didn't hurt that every waitress he hired was under thirty years old and had to be at least a C-cup with a flawless body. If Chef Hue couldn't determine the bra size with his eyes, the palm test usually worked. There wasn't a female employee on the staff that he hadn't slept with. When one seemed to start developing feelings, or would become clingy, he usually replaced her with another. He didn't mind mixing business with pleasure, so long as the latter didn't interfere with the former.

Even though he was able to live a more than comfortable lifestyle, with his own business and home, Chef Hue was not happy. He considered himself a prideful man, and deep down he wanted his success to be based on the quality of his food, not just fake reviews, cheap food, and the big breasts of his waitresses. Chef Hue, despite all he had, was displeased. He wanted to be better. He wanted to be more.

Daily SPECIAL

MEDIOCRE STEW...................................05

Hubert Jenkins was not a religious man. Nevertheless, he did take some time from his intense schedule of cooking, eating, exercising, and fucking to pray to a higher power. After coming home from a poorly attended Thursday night dinner service at the restaurant, Chef Hue prayed for change. To which God? He probably couldn't tell you. He just went to his knees before bed and said "God, please give me the success I deserve..." a bunch of times in a variety of ways, and hoped that one of the deities so many people believed in would take up his plea. As hard as he tried, as much as he learned, he knew that his food wasn't up to par with what he saw on the Food Network.

    He didn't have the imagination or the flair of an Iron Chef. He didn't have the speed and creativity of a Chopped Champion. And he wanted those things. Badly. He knew that, with his basic skillset and lack of creativity, he would have to work incredibly hard for the next twenty years to get to the level that he yearned to reach. Impatient as he was, twenty years was twenty years too long. He would sooner sell his soul to achieve the goal that had eluded him for so long.

Soul for celebrity, he thought with a scoff. *Why not? What's the point of having a soul if you can't attain the things in life that fulfil it?*

With his pedestrian skills, Chef Hue had to accept the fact that he didn't have much of a chance to accomplish his goal of being a young celebrity chef. This bitter acceptance would follow Hubert Jenkins into his dreams that night, plaguing him with nightmares of being cooked inside of a giant pot while his favorite celebrity chefs leaned over the rim and cackled.

Bobby Flay mocked Chef Hue as he sprinkled seasoning on the chef's head. Cat Cora smiled stiffly as she stirred the chef inside of the pot, and Guy Fieri described it all with great exuberance to a cameraman wearing the Grim Reaper's robe. Guy eventually lidded him inside of the cauldron with a high-spirited laugh, leaving Chef Hue to simmer to death, a mediocre stew.

This dream wasn't new to the chef, though it had never felt so fervent, so pressing, so all encompassing, so real. He woke up in the middle of the night, drenched in sweat, swinging his hands upward to fight off the lid to a giant pot that wasn't there. But he felt the heat. He felt it threatening to burn him alive. And he loosed a scream so long and mournful and loud that the security guard in the lobby of his condo called up shortly after, concerned for his wellbeing, citing several calls from his neighbors – those on Chef Hue's floor and on the floors above and below. The embarrassment he felt overtook the fear and foreboding that the dream had instilled in him. He assured the guard that all was okay. A case of night terrors was all.

Before he went back to sleep (with the aid of several Valium – more than he had ever taken in a single swallow), Chef Hue prayed once again. Knowing that the culinary world was bound to eat him alive, Hue prayed to Gods that he didn't quite believe in, Gods that he didn't quite understand.

Perhaps it was the Valium, perhaps it was his being so shaken up by the nightmare that he feared he was bound to reenter as his eyelids grew heavy and his mind grew foggy, but the last thing Chef Hubert Jenkins said before sleep took him was:

"God. Please. She expects me to fail... My mother, she wants me to fail. I put my heart and soul into this. Please let me reach the heights I want to reach. I'd give anything... Everything. Please help me prove her wrong."

The nightmare did not reclaim Hubert, and he slept well for the first time in weeks.

His prayers did not go unnoticed.

BLACK BIRD FEATHERS..............................06

The next day, at the restaurant, Chef Hue still couldn't shake the feeling of failure. He did his usual job of overseeing food prep early in the afternoon, and he watched the front of the restaurant that night, as he typically did on Friday nights when the crowds were a bit larger than normal. The week prior to that particular night, he had received three bad reviews on Yelp. Bad food, bad service, bad restaurant is what the reviews boiled down to. One gold star followed by four white ones always drove Hue up the wall.

    He made sure that his promotion team offset those three bad reviews with twelve good ones. The net difference worked in his favor. There was a slight boost in business that Friday. He should have been counting his blessings, instead he was wishing for more. Wishing that he wasn't one of the many restaurant owners who would never attain anything other than the title of Restaurant Owner. He had once believed he could be all that he dreamed of, now he was disgusted by the fact that he could be nothing more than what he was. Chef Hue looked out at his restaurant from the kitchen window during dinner service; wishing, longing, lamenting.

"Still too many empty seats," Chef Hue mumbled to himself, looking at the nearly filled restaurant.

"What was that, Chef?" Albert, one of Chef Hue's cooks, asked hesitantly. Albert was a hardworking cook with decent culinary skills. In time, Chef Hue believed that Albert could go from decent to good. Unfortunately, Chef Hue didn't feel as though he had the time to sit around and watch anyone blossom. He wanted the quality of food to improve, meaning that the quality of cook had to as well (Chef Hue had conveniently forgotten that he, too, was to blame for the restaurant's umph-less entrees). He turned to Albert distractedly.

"Never mind, Al. Let's just focus on the food, shall we? Seeing as it isn't exactly a madhouse out there, you have time to put your all into each morsel." He gave Albert the cook a look that made the short, overweight, almond-skinned man quiver. It was a look Albert understood all too well. He had seen that look on Chef Hue's face prior to each firing at the restaurant. The chef took a moment to size up the young, bald, tattooed cook as though checking to see who else might fit more suitably behind that apron. Albert had no intention of losing his job. He felt a sudden surge of motivation as he turned from the chef and walked to his station. That night, Albert would have more genuine good reviews about his food from the diners than he had ever received during his one year there.

As Chef Hue continued to peer into his restaurant, he began to reflect on the advice he'd just given the cook. *Focus on the food.* When last had Chef Hue actually focused on the food? The restaurant was gorgeous, a modern design with pristine faux marble floors and thick mahogany tables throughout. The booths were made of fine (fake) Italian leather. The few pieces of artwork that hung elegantly throughout the restaurant were post-modern prints. Art that neither inspired nor offended. Chef Hue thought about the money he had poured into the place in order to get it to look as New Age and trendy as it did. He had thought that turning it from the dive bar it had been when he'd purchased it into the fine dining establishment it now was would be enough to pack the restaurant from bottom to brim every night. He had been hoping to pull in a sophisticated clientele. Instead, he had to settle for loud and boorish students.

Chef Hue hadn't been focused on the food then, and he was beginning to understand that he wasn't really focused on the food now. When last had he taken off his overpriced suit, donned his apron and actually been a Head Chef rather than an owner? It had been a long time. Too long. He had lost his focus some time ago.

He flashed back to his nightmare of being cooked alive by the same celebrity chefs that he one day hoped to call his cohort. The feeling of fear from that dream lit a fire under him similar to the one that had been lit under the cauldron in his nightmare. He took the dream as a sign. He knew that things had to change, that he had to do something other than what he had been doing.

He began to pray again.

"Please, God…"

It was at that moment he saw Her.

His morose thoughts weren't just disrupted, they were dashed.

Thoughts of anything at all halted as he not only lost his focus on the food, he lost focus on everything that wasn't Her. Chef Hue was bewildered. He must have scanned the restaurant at least a hundred times while deep in his thoughts of failure and frustration, how could he possibly have missed seeing *Her*? She sat alone at the corner table that Chef Hue considered to be the best in the house. She demurely sipped a red drink from a cocktail glass. And, as if sensing that Chef Hue had noticed Her, She looked up at him, smiling slightly as they locked eyes – Hers a too-bright blue that reminded him of arctic waters. Those eyes played with him beneath a set of bangs belonging to death-black hair that fell in sheets behind Her shoulders.

Her look alone was enough to leave Chef Hue shaken. He wasn't one to be nervous or intimidated; not since he'd fallen from that stage so many years ago. These days, he had no problem at all approaching beautiful women. And, despite how She rattled him, he knew as soon as his eyes set upon Her that he would have to approach Her. *Have to*. It wasn't a decision that he made, it was a thing he somehow instinctively knew he must do. Like when you know you have to use the bathroom, or you know you have to breathe to continue to live, talking to Her didn't just feel like something he wanted to do, it seemed like an inexorable necessity.

Her smile broadened. Chef Hue felt something tighten in the pit of his stomach, and suddenly the front of his pants seemed far less roomy. She wasn't just beautiful, She was radiant. Literally. Her skin was deeply tanned in a way that made Her seem as if She were glowing. It wasn't the tomato red of a sunburn, rather it was just a hint of red, the loveliest shade Chef Hue had ever seen.

Before Chef Hue even realized that his brain had sent his feet the message to walk, he had slicked back his thick brown hair with the sweat that was beading on his forehead and was at the table standing in front of the raven-haired girl with the rouge skin and the tight, lowcut black dress. He went to say hello, but he drew a blank at any possible greeting. Being that close to Her made the sensation of intrinsic wanting even stronger. He had thought that he wanted to be a celebrity chef more than anything else in his life, now he understood a new level of yearning, one that he had never believed possible. His palms were wet with sweat. The perspiration on his forehead that he had so coolly wiped away was back, threatening now to become streams rather than beads. His stomach clenched, his scrotum tightened around his testicles, drawing them closer to his body, and his knees trembled slightly. He would ask Her to have drinks with him. Yes, that's what he would do.

Then an idea so terrible occurred to Chef Hue that he thought he might fall to his knees and weep right there on the spot. *What if She says no?* Chef Hue shook his head to clear his mind. The thought was too awful to consider. He breathed deeply, trying to calm his mind and relax his rapidly beating heart. He had been standing in front of the black-haired beauty dumbly for nearly an entire minute before he finally, shakily said,

"Hello."

"Hi," she said in response, her voice causing the skin on the back of his neck to tingle. It was lighter fluid over a simmering flame, gravelly without sounding rough or harsh. Chef Hue struggled to keep his composure. Somehow, he managed to.

"May I have a seat?" he asked, trying to project the confidence that he did not posses a shred of in that moment. And he truly did need to have a seat. His legs felt as though they were about to buckle beneath him.

"It's your establishment, isn't it, Mr. Jenkins?" The flirtatious smile never left Her face. "Sit where you please."

Chef Hue sat down in the seat directly in front of Her, grateful to get off of his wobbly legs.

"You know who I am?" he asked, genuinely shocked. He was flattered beyond belief.

"Of course. I've read all of the rave reviews online. I've also seen your bio on the restaurant website. I wanted to see if I should believe what I had read." She paused, sipping Her drink, licking Her lips ever so subtly. "I must say, you're even more handsome in person."

Chef Hue flushed until his skin tone nearly matched Hers.

"Thank you," was all he could muster, before adding, "Are you some sort of food critic?"

"No," She said with a chuckle. "I just appreciate a handsome, ambitious man who can cook a good meal."

Chef Hue beamed. For a moment he was reminded of the day he won the cooking competition that had started all this, the day his mother had died. The day he still considered to be one of the best of his life. Here was another concrete opportunity to prove himself once again. Her validation would be worth far more than any positive online review or compliment to the chef.

"Well then, you've come to the right place," he said, regaining some of his usual confidence. "What would you like to order? I'll make sure to prepare it for you myself, so long as you have a drink with me while you eat it. How does that sound?"

The too-tanned, raven-haired young woman with the crippling blue eyes lifted Her glass to Her lips, finishing the rest of Her drink without taking Her eyes off of Chef Hue. Her lipstick was as black as Her hair.

"Sounds like we have ourselves a deal. I'm Raveena, by the way. Most people call me Raven."

Chef Hue blushed, embarrassed that he hadn't bothered to ask the beauty Her name.

"How rude of me. I apologize, Raveena."

"Call me Raven, please. And there's no need to apologize."

The chef's smile was now so wide that his face hurt. He noticed the black bird feather earrings dangling from Her ears, along with other black bird feathers weaved within her hair, and understood that She must take the nickname seriously.

"Okay, um... Raven. Let me freshen your drink. On the house. What was it?" he asked, looking at her empty cocktail glass.

"I'd be very surprised if you could make one just right for me. Very surprised... and impressed," She said seductively.

"Try me," Chef Hue boasted, his usual confidence nearly fully restored, "I'm full of impressive surprises."

She laughed at his response, exposing perfectly straight, white teeth.

"Fine. It's my absolute favorite drink, so if you ruin it, I'll be very displeased with you. The drink is called *The Gates of Hell*."

She had been correct when She had said She didn't think Chef Hue could make the drink. Chef Hue hadn't even heard of The Gates of Hell (at least not in the non-Biblical sense) before that night, but he wouldn't let Her know that. He smiled, promised he'd be back with the concoction, and trotted off to the bar. A quick Google search on his phone, a brief conversation with his best bartender, Patrick, and five minutes later he was back at Raven's table with The Gates of Hell in his hands. Those hands shook badly, as if the tequila, lemon, lime and cherry brandy mixture within the glass were the components of a ticking time-bomb. If She enjoyed the drink, things would be fine. If She did not enjoy what he presented to Her, his entire world would detonate. She smiled. She sipped. He swooned, having to grab the back of the chair opposite Her to settle his now unreliable legs. She motioned for him to sit. He abided.

"Good job, Mr. Jenkins. You got it just right."

She had gone through four of the drinks before Chef Hue remembered that he'd promised to prepare Her a meal. She drank quickly. So quickly that Chef Hue stopped getting up to get the drinks himself, but instead asked Shelby, one of his more trusted waitresses, to keep a fresh drink coming every ten minutes, relaying to her the importance of ensuring that Patrick made each drink just right. The chef was still on his first glass of wine by the time Raven had swallowed six Gates of Hell cocktails. He was impressed. He was also excited. Chef Hue wasn't above working his charms on a drunk girl. Yet, to his amazement, after knocking back the drinks continuously for thirty minutes, Her composure hadn't changed in the slightest.

On drink eight, Hue whispered to Shelby to bring stronger stuff. Perhaps Patrick was being a bit chintzy with the booze. Raven only smiled as the chef whispered into Shelby's ear. They continued to make small talk as Shelby raced back to the bar, as worried for the disturbingly beautiful woman's liver as she was about losing her job if she didn't do exactly what the chef demanded.

"Is this even legal?" Shelby asked Patrick, blowing a strand of her strawberry blond hair out of her face in exasperation as she repeated the chef's instructions. Patrick only shrugged, indicating that they both knew enough about Chef Hue to stay out of his business. She grimaced, remembering what she'd had to do to get last year's holiday bonus. Legality wasn't a top priority for her employer.

Shelby returned with the next round of drinks to the table Chef Hue and The Red Lady occupied. With the drinks made double stiff, Raven drank four more. Twelve drinks in and not a slur or stutter. Chef Hue watched with eyes as wide as dinner plates. His astonishment was mirrored by the expression on Shelby's face each time she would bring another drink. Even a few of the patrons were beginning to take notice.

"Do you always drink so much?" Hubert inquired, not wanting to seem rude, but too curious to avoid asking.

"Do you always drink so little?" She responded without hesitation. Her smile didn't fade, and Her ice-blue eyes stared directly into him as She downed Her thirteenth drink. Chef Hue felt heat rise to the top of his head, as it usually did when he was made to feel foolish. Unlike his mother, he wasn't much of a drinker, but he didn't intend to look like a pushover when compared to a woman who couldn't have weighed more than one hundred and forty pounds. So, when She started on drink fourteen, Hubert Jenkins started on whiskey shots one, two and three.

CALF'S BRAINS AND COW TONGUE 07

By shot seven (drink sixteen for Raven), Chef Hue once again remembered that he had promised to make his lovely companion a meal. He asked Her what She wanted to eat, promising Her anything, regardless of what was on the menu. She smiled even wider, exposing more perfect teeth, nearly rupturing Hubert's heart at a glance. She motioned with the index finger of Her right hand for him to lean in closer.

He leaned in over the table, now inches away from Her. At this proximity he was sweating profusely, not just because of his nerves, but because Her tanned skin seemed to radiate heat. She whispered Her order into his cheek, Her lips grazing the clean-shaven skin of his face as She talked. He shifted his hardening penis with his hand, hoping the motion would remain unnoticed by both The Red Lady and his other patrons.

When She was done, he sat back, allowing his blood to start flowing from his crotch back to other areas of his body. He tried not to look surprised by what She had asked for as he slowly stood, slightly hunched, and walked toward the kitchen. He was relieved to get a chance to stop drinking and start cooking, though he experienced a forlorn feeling, which he could only describe as a sense of mourning, that increased the further away from Her he got.

He turned back on his booze-and-lust-wobbled legs at least ten times between Her table and the kitchen door forty feet away. It was as though he was worried She would vanish as suddenly as She had appeared, leaving an irreparable hole in his being. Each time he looked back, She was still there, still smiling at him with Her ethereal glow and gleaming blue eyes. He took one last look before walking through the kitchen doors. With the doors behind him, separating him from Her, he felt lost. Helpless. Yet he composed himself enough to prepare what She had asked for, despite how unusual Her order was.

Her appetite matched Her thirst. The chef had promised to make Her a meal, imagining a simple entrée. He hadn't anticipated Her ordering a personal buffet, including items that weren't in his kitchen at all. He found he didn't mind what he normally would have considered to be a massive inconvenience as he gathered his herbs and spices from the racks and pulled a variety of fresh meat from the fridge. It took Hue over an hour and a half to have everything prepared. It would have taken longer if Raven hadn't asked for much of her meal to be done rare, blue in some cases.

When that hour and a half had passed (a period of time during which Chef Hue had run to the kitchen window every few minutes to make sure She was still there), he needed two waitresses to help him with Her order. They carried three plates each. He carried the final two. They gently placed the eight plates in front of Raven, then backed away slowly, watching, wondering if She would actually eat it all. It was the same fascination one has when watching a pack of wolves devour a caribou. They were disturbed and intrigued all at once.

It wasn't just Chef Hue and his wait staff watching, the other patrons had stopped their own dining to admire the small woman taking on the impossibly large meal, taking photos and video of the spectacle before them.

The Red Lady didn't mind the attention. Raven knew that they wouldn't remember any of this minutes after She walked out of the restaurant. The photos and video that had been taken would appear blurry and distorted beyond recognition wherever they were saved or uploaded. With that in mind, she decided to put on a show of devouring what had been placed upon the eight plates.

One plate held a sixteen-ounce sirloin steak, cooked (if you could call it that) blue rare. Another held a fourteen-ounce bone-in rib eye steak, also blue. Another a sixteen-ounce T-bone steak, rare. Two of the plates were piled high with an array of uncooked sea food: shrimp, mussels, oysters, clams, and squid. One plate contained two fillets of salmon prepared with lemon juice in the style of a ceviche, though without the appropriate time needed for it to marinate and become a true ceviche. Chef Hue had mentioned that to Her. She had only smiled and told him that She didn't mind.

The remaining two plates that Chef Hue held were the most difficult of the items to prepare. Mainly because neither of the items were on *A Lovely Hue*'s menu, and therefore were not in his kitchen at all. Chef Hue had sent a waitress to the French restaurant a block and a half away to get the calf's brains and cow tongue he set down in front of Her on the plate in his left hand. He'd had to send another runner to the neighboring state of Kentucky to find a Cajun restaurant that served crawdaddies. The chef had to pay extra to get the restaurant to sell live crawfish to his waitress. Those two-dozen or so crawfish were still crawling around on the deep-set dinner plate in his hand as he walked over to present the last of Her order. He had lost a few on the way to Her table from the kitchen, as some had chosen to dive overboard rather than await their fate.

The rest of the crawfish began to scurry off of the plate as soon as it was set down, but Raven made sure none of them got too far. At this point, everyone in the dining area had their eyes on The Red Lady, watching in astonishment as She grabbed the critters and shoved them in Her mouth by the fistful, sucking and slurping the juice out of their shells before swallowing the exoskeletons whole. They wiggled and writhed as they struggled to escape their deaths. None would get away.

She then turned Her attention to the slightly less alive items on Her table, attacking the cuts of beef next.

She ate each steak in two bites.

Chef Hue could have sworn that Her jaw unhinged as She dropped the last of the T-bone into Her gaping mouth, bone included. She didn't use the utensils that were in front of Her, She was more of a hands-on girl.

After the steaks were devoured, Raven raised each plate to Her mouth and licked at the myoglobin that remained on the dishes, locking eyes with Chef Hue as She did so. Chef Hue noticed that Her tongue was unusually long and dark, almost as black as her hair. It seemed to descend at least two inches below Her chin as She let it work on the residue on the plates. A chill ran up his spine as he thought of what that tongue could do to him.

Hue should have been alarmed. He should have been disgusted by Her savagery. Instead, he was aroused, and very thankful that he was still wearing the apron he had used to prepare Her meal so that no one could see just how aroused he was. She could sense it, however.

Raven had always had a keen sense of when she was wanted.

Needed.

Yearned for.

She went to work on the rest of the meal, leaning over on the table, eating with Her mouth atop each plate like a pig would eat from a trough. And, for a horrifying moment, Hubert Jenkins thought of his mother, face down, dead in her personal trough of spam and ramen. He cringed as his cock hardened further. But Raven was not merely eating, She was *vacuuming* the food into Her mouth and down Her throat. Chef Hue looked away for a moment, as he was distracted by a flutter of wings and a flurry of black shapes that flew across his peripheral vision. For a moment he thought he saw several large black birds landing on various tables, pecking at the dinners of his patrons.

The Chef expected outrage and outbursts. Gearing himself to avert a meltdown, Chef Hue turned full-on toward the birds he had just witnessed swooping around his restaurant... and saw only his patrons, unperturbed, their attention fixedly on the black-haired beauty. Their dinners unmolested. No birds in sight. Perplexed, Chef Hue turned his attention back toward The Red Lady.

She was finished with all eight plates, and it had barely taken her that number of minutes to do so. She sat back, looked at Shelby the waitress, and then looked at one of the male restaurant goers a few tables over who had been raptly recording Her performance. The two froze under The Red Lady's stare before they both dropped to their knees and crawled slowly toward Raven, rising up like dogs expecting a treat when they reached Her.

Raven leaned to each of them and allowed them to lick the juices from the seafood and beef off her face. When they were done, they simply stood, turned, and walked back to where they had been before they'd been summoned, continuing on as though nothing had happened.

The restaurant goer who had just been licking Raven's face sat back in front of his boyfriend, neither of them looked as though they'd noticed he had ever risen from his seat.

Shelby collected the empty glasses from a nearby table, took another drink order, and walked back to the bar nonchalantly.

Chef Hue was ready to explode.

"Check, please!" Raven said to no one in particular, and with no intent to pay.

Five minutes later, She and Chef Hue were in the back of a cab on their way to his condo. By that time, the patrons had gone back to their conversations, none of which featured mention of a slightly red young woman devouring eight plates of raw food, or the sensual act of the two people licking her face clean.

They talked about what they talked about over any other meal on a Friday at *A Lovely Hue*: upcoming exams, world events, who was fucking whom, the usual.

The wait staff cleared Raven's table, not quite remembering who had sat there, or where their boss had gone. Shelby was especially pissed that whoever had been there had taken off without bothering to pay.

Daily SPECIAL

OUROBOROS..**08**

When She caused him to orgasm, Chef Hue didn't just come, he went. Then came and went, again and again.

The feeling was so exquisite that he thought he was going to die. And if he had perished in that moment, he was certain he would have been just fine with that. What else of worth could come after a feeling such as this? He knew that he would never find physical pleasure as great as what he had just experienced as long as he lived. He began to weep as The Red Lady dismounted from him.

Rolling onto his side on his disheveled bed, he watched Her through the blur of his tears. He was out of breath from their encounter, from the sensations, from what She had done *to* him as much as with him.

The experience was so much more than sex. So much greater than any singular experience he'd ever had. When he was inside of Her, he felt like he was outside of himself. And when he released into Her, it was as though he were allowed a glimpse of everything inside of the Universe at once. For a fraction of a moment, he saw things... impossible things. The worlds outside of this world. Galaxies imploding, galaxies being birthed, a road shaped like infinity that coursed through it all. He saw life beyond his imagination, creatures that his brain could not make sense of, and he was crestfallen when those images became dim to him as his climax diminished.

He could only watch as She got up from his bed. He didn't have enough air in him left to tell Her not to go. She put on Her clothes, slowly, sensually. It didn't take Her very long, She had only been wearing a skin tight black dress with nothing beneath it. He sighed as the dress slid down over the two dimples on Her lower back. He gasped as the dress covered Her bottom, hiding what he was so eager to enjoy once more.

As She adjusted Her hair, he took note of the tattoo below Her neck, just between Her shoulder blades. It was the number eight inked onto her skin sideways, with two equal sized loops forming the digit. It was drawn in clean black outlines, Her red skin filling its hollows. Within the tattooed eight were six star-like shapes, three in the left loop of the eight, three in the right. He felt an unease in the pit of his stomach as he stared at the marking. The longer he looked at it, the more the sensation swelled. The figure eight entranced him, and, for a moment, he thought he saw it pulse from Her skin and begin to move. It was then he noticed that it wasn't just a figure eight, it was an ouroboros – a snake swallowing itself; its body forming two concentric loops.

It *was* moving.

The snake tattooed on her skin slithered in a macabre, self-mutilating motion around the six stars on The Red Lady's upper back. The longer he watched it, the more entranced he felt. For a brief moment, he felt as though he were being lifted from himself, becoming an onlooker.

He saw Her, he saw himself watching Her and, for another brief moment, he wasn't just looking at the tattoo on Her back, he was looking into it. Inside of the loops of the snake's body, he was shown what lay within.

Just a glimpse.

It was a vision that so rocked his senses he flinched at its approach. When it hit him, what he saw was fire. There were hands above those flames, fingers extended, palms out and upward. Those hands were connected to arms that waved to and fro in a frenzied, relentless dance. The faces which owned the appendages contorted in an expression that Chef Hue – still racked with the aftermath of his climax – mistook to be pleasure.

Then Her hair fell, covering the tattoo and ending the odd sensation within Chef Hue as well as the vision that had come with it, but not diminishing how badly he craved Her return to his bed. The Red Lady turned to him, sensing his lust, and flashed him one last smile before She walked out of his bedroom and out of his life.

"You'll get what you want, Hubert Jenkins," She called to him from the hallway, "Just make sure you actually want it."

His apartment door closed behind Raven with a bang. He didn't know what She had meant, but he would in time.

At that moment, listening to the echo of the jarring bang of his condo door closing, knowing that She was gone, potentially forever, he felt hideously empty. Like something inside of him had exited along with Her. The experience was too much for him. Hubert fell asleep on his side, naked, wheezing and weeping.

Daily SPECIAL

LOBSTER BISQUE..**09**

He woke up late the next day. Very late. So late that it was mid-afternoon.

"Fuck!" Chef Hue shouted as he looked at the large clock on his bedroom wall. He jumped out of bed quickly in an attempt to get ready and rush to the restaurant. But when his feet hit the ground his legs buckled beneath him. He fell to the floor in a heap. His body was weak, his head was throbbing. He groaned at his discomfort and confusion. His initial thought was that it was a hangover; then he remembered that he had stopped drinking when he had begun to prepare the meal. *Her* meal. He had only been slightly buzzed when they'd gotten to the apartment, and he had been too busy being consumed by Her to even give thought to another drink. No, it wasn't a hangover. It was Her.

She had drained him so thoroughly that, even after sleeping in six hours later than he normally did, he was still feeling the effects of Her. Chef Hue dragged himself up, using his bed to do so, until he stood shakily, waiting for his strength to return.

It wasn't like him to sleep through his alarm. It wasn't like him to sleep in at all. The alarm clock was a precaution, a failsafe, almost a novelty item. Usually, Hue would be up no later than nine in the morning, regardless of how late he'd gone to bed the night prior.

When he felt steady enough to move, he shuffled over to his cell phone which lay face up on his end table. The phone also acted as his backup alarm, and it was off. Pressing the power button repeatedly, Hue understood that it wasn't just he that was drained of energy that morning. Unable to call his staff to find out how the Saturday afternoon shift was going, Hue, in a panic, grabbed the first pair of pants and the first shirt he saw, quickly put on a pair of shoes (his socks were still on from the night before), and ran out of the apartment as fast as his unsteady legs could carry him.

Chef Hue was still out of sorts ten minutes later when he arrived at *A Lovely Hue Restaurant and Bar*.

If his first surprise of the day had been waking up hours after he usually would, his second surprise was the vintage chalkboard on an easel just outside of the restaurant. A chalkboard that he hadn't permitted to be set up outside of his establishment. He approached the easel, confused, annoyed. His annoyance increased to anger when he saw what was written upon it. The chalkboard read:

DAILY SPECIAL

LOBSTER BISQUE

HAVE A BOWL
FREE OF CHARGE

☺

Hue frowned at the sign, pursing his lips as he was wont to do when he felt his authority had been challenged. The message was written in his hand, though he was certain he hadn't written it. Nor would he ever give anything away free of charge.

He approached the front doors not knowing what to expect next. He had left the restaurant in the hands of his staff before, though he had never done so without leaving incredibly detailed, explicit instructions as to what was to go on from the moment the front door was unlocked until the moment the restaurant was closed for the evening. Trust was never Chef Hue's strong suit. And on the long list of things that Chef Hue did not trust, his employees were near the top, below the government and above women.

With a deep feeling of unease, Chef Hue opened the double doors to his restaurant, expecting chaos. When he walked in and saw that the restaurant was in a state it had never been in during the two years he had owned it, he was stunned.

The dining area was buzzing.

Though the house wasn't entirely packed, it was certainly fuller than it had ever been on a Saturday afternoon. Unable to trust what he was seeing, Chef Hue rushed to the bar section of his establishment.

The atmosphere there was as electric as the dining area. There wasn't a person in the entire building without a smile on their face. If they weren't smiling, they were laughing.

And in front of every single one of the patrons was a soup bowl, wiped clean.

Chef Hue had to double check this as he walked back from the bar to the dining area. Yes, each customer had an identical silver bowl with indecipherable red etching on the outside of it in front of them. Each bowl was emptied. Some of the clients had traces of food smeared around their mouths, on their cheeks and chins, as though they had lapped up the contents of the bowls in front of them like dogs – bowls which Chef Hue didn't recognize as his own.

There was an eerie feeling in the electric air that now filled his restaurant. Like something was out of place. Like *everything* was out of place. Upon noticing him, the waitresses stared with wide, disbelieving eyes. They too felt the eerie essence permeating the air of the restaurant. The chef sprinted as fast as he could to the kitchen to find out exactly what was going on.

When Chef Hue entered the kitchen, he was met with surprises three and four of the day. Surprise the third was that the only one of his kitchen staff who was present was Albert, the so-so cook. Albert was pacing back and forth like a man waiting for a piece of bad news he knew he couldn't handle.

"What's going on here, Al? Why the Hell are all of those people getting free bisque? That shit's not cheap you know! And where is everyone?" Hue was screaming by the end of the second question, his head still hurting from whatever it was that had happened the night before.

The memory of what had happened the previous night seemed to have fallen out of his head nearly entirely somewhere between his condo and the restaurant. What remained of his memory made little sense: pools of frozen blue water, a red wave rolling atop him, threatening to extinguish him with its heat.

A snake... a snake devouring itself.

It was Chef Hue who was now red in the face. He had bits of spittle in his goatee. His brown hair was disheveled. Hue pushed one sweaty, shaky hand through it to get it out of his eyes, and waited for Albert's response. Albert stopped pacing. He looked sick to his stomach, and, for a disastrous moment, Hue believed his second in command was going to spew all over the floor. Instead, Albert reached into his pocket, withdrew a piece of paper folded many times over, and handed it to the chef. The paper read:

Al,

Send the kitchen staff home for the week. With pay.

Remove the menu from the front of the house. We will only be serving a daily special from now on. I will write the special on the chalkboard outside each morning before we open. Today will be lobster bisque. You can find the bisque inside of the pot on the main stove. New plates and bowls are in the storage room. Today's special will be FREE OF CHARGE. Expect a lot of hungry mouths to feed! Just keep dishing out while the waitresses do their job. And don't worry, we won't run out.

The note was unsigned, but was clearly Hue's writing. Now it was Chef Hue's turn to pace. He scratched his head as he walked back and forth. Was it possible that he had written the message on the chalkboard as well as the note to Albert? No. All of it was nonsense. None of it was possible.

The absurdity was increased when Chef Hue looked at the main cooker and saw the fourth surprise of that day: an antique-looking medium-sized cast iron pot. It sat indifferently on the front left burner of the stove. The pot was dented and dinged all over. On the side of the pot facing Chef Hue and Albert the Cook was an etching: small black shapes on the gray of the pot. Chef Hue had to stare at the design for nearly a minute before it became clear to him that the black shapes were six black birds.

Ravens.

The word made his head swim.

The antique pot looked preposterous against the background of the modern kitchen. Chef Hue looked all around the kitchen as if in search of something, then he laughed despite the increasingly odd circumstances.

"You mean to tell me that *this* little pot fed all of *those* people?"

Chef Hue thought back to the number of red trimmed bowls he had seen as he'd run through his restaurant.

It was impossible.

Everything he remembered from the last twenty-four hours seemed literally unbelievable. Albert looked sullenly from the pot to his boss and back again, as if not wanting to believe what he was about to affirm.

"Yes," he whispered, coarsely. "It never ends..." He continued to stammer before regaining his composure. "How do you do it, Chef?"

The chef didn't have an answer to that. The note was in his font, however, much like the sign outside, he didn't recall writing it. Nor had he ever seen that medieval-looking pot.

He felt like he had to approach it. He stepped softly, cautiously, lifting the lid with the care a bomb squad technician takes when handling an explosive. He wasn't sure what to expect. What he got was the second knee wobbling experience of that day.

The aroma that floated from the reddish-orange stew was enough to nearly entrance the chef. He had never smelled anything so wonderful in all his years.

"Jesus Christ," Chef Hue murmured. And, as if sensing the presence of the chef, the half empty pot of orange-red soup began to bubble, then boil, despite the burner beneath it being off. Chunks of radiant lobster and bright green chives that Chef Hue hadn't seen just a moment before rose to the top. It took all his willpower to peel his eyes away from the pot of bisque and look at Albert.

"Have you tried this, Al?" Chef Hue asked quietly, hesitantly, salivating at this point.

"Yes, Chef. It's the most beautiful thing I've ever tasted. If not for the fact that the pot is bottomless I woulda eaten it all myself... God knows I tried. I don't know how you did this. I don't know how this is happening." Albert's voice was beyond distressed. He sounded lost. Dazed.

Chef Hue whirled all the way around until he was facing his cook.

"Bottomless?" was all he could utter as he finally began to understand what was happening. Understand, yes, but not believe.

Al could only nod, watery-eyed, as the chef gave him a once over. The cook was nearly covered in red-orange stains. Albert's stomach was visibly bulging behind his apron, his breathing was ragged. Chef Hue wondered just how much of the free bisque his cook had eaten.

"Nonsense," Chef Hue said. It wasn't an admonishment, necessarily. It was more of an admission that nothing was adding up. Chef Hue wasn't ready to believe that some magical pot had appeared and had fed an entire restaurant as well as a gluttonous cook. The pot boiled harder, as if to change his mind. The aroma floated up to Chef Hue, teasing him, calling him to take a taste.

Shaking from the peculiarity of all that was that day, he grabbed a wooden spoon from a nearby drawer. He placed the long-handled implement into the now full pot – not only had the amount of soup within the pot doubled in size, the bisque had somehow gone from a boil to a simmer all on its own. The chef would have liked to believe that he was only trying the bisque from the foreign pot because Al had confirmed the substance not to be toxic. However, the truth was that even if he had been told he was about to drink poison in the form of soup, Chef Hue wouldn't have been able to stop himself from doing so. The scent alone had seeped into his head and wrapped around his nodes and synapses. He shivered from fear. He shuddered from ecstasy.

He put the spoon full of bisque to his lips and sipped. He had to brace himself against the stove to stop from falling over. As marvelous as the smell was, the taste was better by tenfold. Chef Hubert Jenkins slowly allowed his wobbly legs to give way beneath him. He dropped to his knees as if in reverence of the still too-hot-for-tasting bisque he had just sampled from the iron pot. The fact that he had burned his mouth was inconsequential. The taste! The flavor! It was better than any food he had ever experienced!

He threw the spoon across the room. Without thinking, Chef Hue stood, grabbed one of the red trimmed silver bowls from the nearby countertop, and used it as a makeshift shovel. He reached into the pot, getting as much of the bisque into the bowl as possible. He then poured the contents into his face, ignoring the heat of the substance as it splashed and dribbled down his cheeks, chin and neck. After chugging three bowls full of bisque, and noticing that the contents of the pot hadn't decreased, Hue turned to Albert and asked,

"How is this even possible?"

Albert grimaced as though he was scared of the question.

"Dunno, Chef. But I've been serving and eating lobster bisque from that same pot for the last four hours."

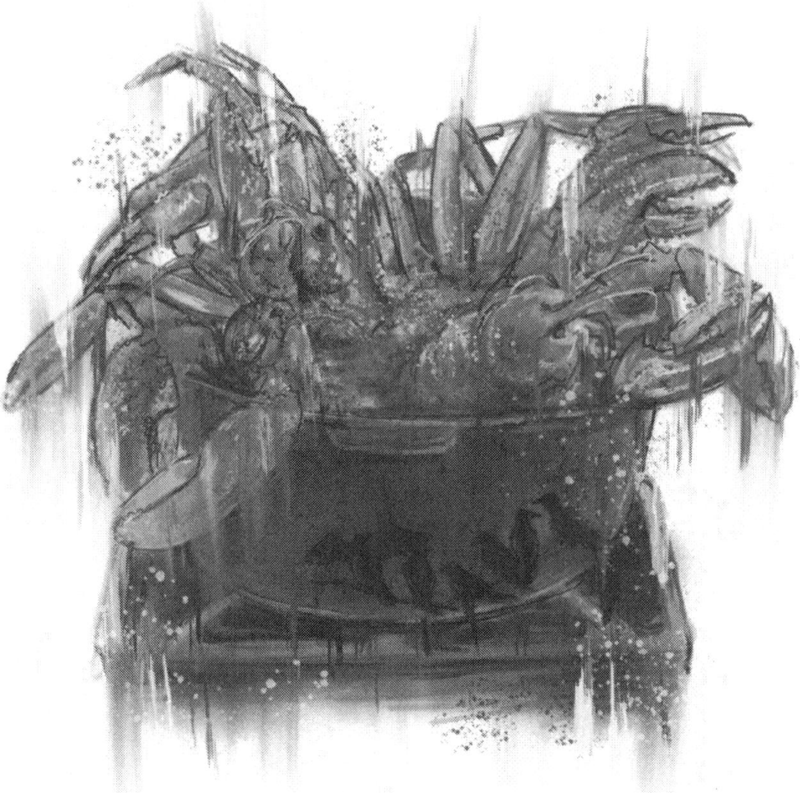

Daily SPECIAL

MACARONI BATHED IN CHEESE......................**10**

It was the same the day after.

Chef Hue arrived (this time he was punctual) ready to cook. The bisque he had eaten still lingered on his taste buds, dancing with him, encouraging him to be better, to cook with more passion, to pay more attention to the little details needed to get any kind of recognition in the culinary community. Though he began to realize that his skills might not be necessary when he saw the chalkboard was still in front of his restaurant, even though he had taken it inside the night before and locked it in the storage room. He had been the last to leave the previous night. He was the first to arrive this morning. Yet, there the chalkboard stood.

He blanched. It read:

DAILY SPECIAL

SOUTHERN
STYLE
MAC & CHEESE

$5 A PLATE

Again, the hand was his. He shook his head and walked into the empty establishment. The patrons hadn't left until an hour after close the night before. Many were demanding more free bisque. Chef Hue had served out the delicacy (having to stop himself from eating directly from their bowls) soup kitchen style; patrons had lined up at the kitchen window, foregoing the wait-staff as Hue handed out bowl after bowl, turning away those who he could identify were coming back for seconds. When he had finally declared that last call for soup was up, and the doors would be closed at 2 a.m., physical violence nearly broke out.

Chef Hue was able to settle things down by telling the aggressors there would be more wonderful food the next day, though he hadn't at that point known how he was going to compete with the bisque in the Unending Pot. Now, as he walked into his restaurant and smelled the mac and cheese in the air, he understood that the bisque could be rivaled.

Chef Hue followed his nose all the way to the kitchen, where he found the cast iron pot sitting in the same spot it had been the day before, with slow tendrils of steam rising from beneath the lid. He walked warily toward it, not knowing what to expect. Not knowing if it would even open for him. He and Albert had tried to toss out the pot the night prior, to no avail. The two men could not make the pot budge. They had tried for half an hour, pushing, pulling, hitting, attempting to knock it over, but the pot seemed to weigh ten thousand pounds.

After a long, sweaty period of time, the men had decided they would scoop out and throw away the addictive substance inside of the pot. The pot, and everything that had happened that day, was too unnerving for either man to handle rationally. As much as they wanted to keep it, and the bisque it had created, they felt it would be prudent to rid themselves of the creepy cast iron cookware and its contents before the very idea of it drove them mad.

The plan had been to clean it out and move on since they couldn't throw the thing away entirely. But, when Hue had attempted to lift the lid off the pot, it wouldn't budge. Again, they had struggled. They had attached a rope to the knob at the center of the lid and both men had engaged in a tug of war with the cookware. The struggle was preposterous. By the end of it all, both men were sore and sweating, and Albert looked as though he had seen several ghosts.

Like most adults, Albert's mind wasn't designed to handle things he couldn't understand. Things that didn't fit neatly within the boundaries of all he had believed he knew about logic and reason and what should and shouldn't be able to happen. Albert was facing something impossible, the sort of impossible thing that has a way of shattering even the healthiest of minds. Albert had stopped believing in spooks and ghosts and creatures that went bump in the night early into his teenage years. Yet he had stood in Hue's kitchen, shaking, swearing, sweating, staring wide eyed at the boogeyman himself, come in the form of an old cast iron pot. He had never been more afraid in all his years.

Chef Hue wound up sending the young cook home, fearing he would suffer a nervous breakdown. Chef Hue, too, had been quite shaken. After Albert left, the chef had tried to lift the lid and the pot once more before he resigned himself to the fact that neither would budge. Making sure that all the burners were off, the chef had gone home feeling a great deal of unease and trepidation. He hadn't thought he would have been able to sleep, but the stress of that day was the only sleeping aid he would need as it turned out. He passed out shortly after laying fully clothed on his bed. He had expected nightmares, but his sleep had been pitch black and dreamless.

Now, although steam lazily danced out from beneath the closed lid of the pot, Chef Hue could see that the burner beneath it was off. He stepped toward it with apprehension. He went to lift the lid, not knowing if it would be stuck as it had been the night before, but suspecting that it would give freely. This time, Hue was the only person in the large establishment, and though he'd opened up the restaurant hundreds of times on his own, he had never done so while experiencing such overwhelmingly surreal feelings of terror and confusion.

The lid lifted, the vapor from inside of the pot hitting him in the face and rocking his senses. His nostrils flared, he began to sweat, his mouth moistened, and his cock hardened as he looked at the contents within. Elbows of macaroni bathed in cheese and surrounded by thick cut pieces of bacon and green onions sat awaiting the chef. There was a dusting of breadcrumbs, cayenne and black pepper spread delicately throughout the mixture. The chef knew those crumbs would never go soggy, no matter how long they sat in the pot. Though they wouldn't have to sit there long.

Hue grabbed a fork without thinking. He dipped into the contents of the pot and watched in wonder as cheese stretched between the pot and his fork. The chef's nose was sharp enough to know that there were at least three kinds of cheeses on his fork at that moment: white cheddar, asiago, romano, and perhaps another he could not quite identify. He took a bite, unmindful of the heat of the substance. His craving was greater than the burn he would receive once the morsels were in his mouth.

Chef Hue's senses nearly unhinged when he finally tasted the southern delicacy. His eyes began to water with a feeling he could only equate with joy. He had to grasp the edge of the stove for the second time in two days, bracing himself as the food worked its magic upon him. At that moment, the chef understood that if the pot continued to produce, as it had over the last two days, he would be rich, his celebrity would be attained. He beamed at the idea of it. Then Hue struggled against himself to lid the pot. A weaker man may have climbed upon the cool stove and eaten from the pot until his stomach exploded. However, Hubert Jenkins of the singular focus understood that the pot was to be tasted from, perhaps a small portion here and there, but he could not allow himself to binge as he had the previous day. Not if he hoped to maintain his mind.

Albert showed up an hour later. Half an hour late. They should have begun prepping for Sunday lunch service when he walked in, still ashen, still shaky, looking like a man who hadn't slept in days. Usually, Chef Hue would have been furious. But usually, Chef Hue wouldn't have been preoccupied by a pot that had seemingly prepared his food for him before he had even walked through the door. He was still trying to attribute some sort of logical explanation to the situation. Maybe someone had snuck in and cooked the food before he'd walked into the restaurant... Maybe someone was discretely funneling food into the pot somehow... But who? And why? And how the fuck?

He had been staring at the pot with his hands on his hips, eliminating one farfetched possibility after the other, when Albert walked into the kitchen.

"Hey, Al. You're late." He said this without his usual vigor, disdain or conviction.

"I wasn't gonna come in at all," Albert muttered. "I was gonna quit all out. But I had to see that pot again. I need to know that I ain't losin' it, chef." Albert walked hesitantly toward the stove, approached the pot, and removed the lid. The steam hit him the same way it had hit Chef Hue earlier. Al went visibly weak. He placed both hands on the handles of the pot. At first Chef Hue thought Albert was doing this in order to brace himself, until he saw that Al was trying to pull the pot over the edge of the stove in order to upset the contents within it.

"NO!" Hue screamed. He went to stop Al from doing what he planned to do. But there was no need. The pot wouldn't budge. It was Al's turn to yell in protest.

"This ain't right! This ain't normal! This ain't NATURAL! This ain't POSSIBLE!"

When he understood that he still couldn't throw the pot onto the floor, Albert lifted the lid and threw it across the room. It hit the far wall with a crash, giving Albert a sense of satisfaction that he would only truly appreciate years later, in his prison cell, when he reflected upon the insanity of what had occurred because of that pot. But, for the time being, he only thought about not allowing the chef to serve what was in the little cauldron (that was how he had begun to think of it as he'd tossed and turned in his bed the entire night prior).

Albert thrust his hands into the pot, and though his hands burned hot, he shoveled out the contents and threw them on the floor, scoop after scoop. At first the chef went to stop his cook, but Albert turned on him with the eyes of a rabid animal, and Chef Hue was certain that if he got too close this man gone wild would leave him without significant chunks of his flesh. Chef Hue only watched, not knowing what to do. This went on for five very fascinating minutes. Despite Albert's scooping and throwing of the mac and cheese, the pot's contents never diminished. What was inside was never reduced. Its levels never dipped.

Not even slightly.

The more food that Albert threw on the floor, the stronger the aroma inside of the kitchen became. Chef Hue fought against the temptation of falling to his hands and knees and cleaning up the mess with his tongue. He instead covered his nose and mouth with a cloth, hoping that would help diminish some of the craving. Albert, however, did not have the good sense to do as the chef had done. He became overwhelmed by the very thing he was protesting.

Chef Hue never had to tell Albert to clean up the mess, because Albert dropped down to all fours and began eating the piles of macaroni, cheese and bacon off of the ground, licking the floor clean. And, once the floor was spotless, he turned to his own hands.

Chef Hue's eyes bulged as he saw Albert nearly swallow his entire right hand in an attempt to lick off the food that was on it. Albert went to work on his hands like a dog to a sparsely covered bone. Chef Hue watched in fascinated horror as Albert ripped and chewed at his skin in an attempt to get all of the flavor. It wasn't until blood began to leak from his tattered fingers that Albert truly understood what had happened. It wasn't until Albert looked at the blistered and torn skin of his hands that he knew he had failed. That he had been beaten... by a pot.

He began to wail.

Albert fell onto his belly, his face upon the floor as he writhed in pain, weeping, screaming, and babbling incoherently as he did so.

His cook's wailing seemed to snap Chef Hue out of his trance. The chef walked toward his cook, then stepped over Albert's quaking body on his way to the pot. It was still full, much to the chef's delight. He turned to Albert the cook, who was now kneeling back on his haunches whimpering over his bloody and ruined hands. Chef Hue shuddered at the mess his cook had become, but his decision was clear as he thought about the contents of the pot behind him. His voice was muffled by the cloth that covered the lower half of his face as he spoke.

"It's probably best that you leave, Al," Chef Hue said coldly. "Thank you for all of your help."

Daily SPECIAL

STUFFED PORTOBELLO MUSHROOMS 11

The pot never stopped producing. Each day, Chef Hue would come into work nervous that the chalkboard with the daily special written upon it would be gone. Each day, he was pleased to see it was still there.

There was no rhyme or reason as to what the special would be on any particular day. Regardless of what food Chef Hue thought of or wished for the night before, or on his drive to the restaurant, the food item would be different. Random. Beef stroganoff on the third day, spaghetti and meatballs on the seventh, tamales on the eighth, ratatouille the tenth, chicken soup on the twelfth. It could have been anything, which made promoting the next day's special impossible for Chef Hue. He learned very quickly, however, that promoting his restaurant was no longer a necessity, because every single thing the pot churned out was delicious. Maddeningly, incomprehensively, unbelievably delicious. Within weeks the word about "Chef Hue's Daily Special" spread all over town, then to the surrounding cities, and eventually to most of the country.

It had started with the chalkboard on the easel outside of his restaurant stating that the lobster bisque would be free on the first day that it and the pot had shown up. The chalkboard stated that patrons should be charged five dollars per plate for the mac and cheese on the second day. On the third day, the beef stroganoff was priced at seven dollars and fifty cents per serving. That was the last suggested pricing that the chalkboard would make, but Chef Hue didn't need the strategy drawn out for him. He simply had to increase the prices as his restaurant's popularity increased.

So long as the pot is doing its thing, they will pay. They will eat, and they will beg to pay more, the chef told himself.

He began to write the prices on the chalkboard once it told him and the rest of the world what the daily special would be. After the fourth day, the chef was charging forty dollars a plate for each special, regardless of what it was. By day twelve, people were gladly paying fifty dollars for a bowl of chicken noodle soup.

He had to double his wait and bar staff, though he never hired another cook to replace Al. When his kitchen staff had returned from their paid week off, he dismissed them all. He didn't need them so long as the pot continued to cook. Nor did he want his secret to be shared with anyone else, including the rest of his employees who didn't work in the kitchen. Chef Hue personally placed each plate in the order window himself. None of his employees were allowed into the kitchen. No one was allowed to try the food under any circumstances. The fewer questions about Hue's cooking process, the better.

As incentive for their apathy, *A Lovely Hue*'s waitresses and bartenders were soon paid twice the amount their counterparts in other establishments were making, as well as the tips they received from the always satisfied patrons, which nearly doubled their newly inflated salaries. They made more than enough to not ask any questions. Go to work, grab the plate, get the drink, put it on the table, get paid, go home, and repeat.

Just three months after the pot had mysteriously appeared in Hue's kitchen, *A Lovely Hue Restaurant and Bar* became known internationally for its amazing daily specials. People would travel to Cincinnati from all over the world for the specific purpose of trying the food the restaurant produced. Customers lined up all the way down the block and around the corner for the daily special. The waitstaff were always certain there wouldn't be enough food to feed them all. They were always incorrect about that. Still, each day, they prepared themselves to disappoint those waiting outside. The staff also prepared themselves for outrage on a daily basis, as they had previously seen the reaction of customers who had been told that feeding time was over. They prepared themselves for violence, many of them often thinking back to the night before the very first of those monumental lineups.

There had been a stabbing that night.

A knifing. Over who would have the last plate of stuffed Portobello mushrooms the chef had placed at the order window after declaring last call for food. Five patrons had approached the single plate containing ten mushroom caps stuffed with spinach, pepperoni, ground beef, two cheeses, and a variety of spices. The chef had watched as they began to bicker, then scream, then, eventually, throw hands, none of them even considering that there were enough mushroom caps to give them two to a person. Each of them wanted all ten.

The Chef stood in the kitchen, looking through the order window with a gleam in his eye, intrigued by all of this, much as he had been when he watched Albert the cook chewing upon his own hands.

The customer closest to the plate when the melee began had been a portly, middle aged white woman with short, graying hair. The others punched and screamed and scratched at each other while this woman, who would otherwise go unnoticed in any other location on any other day, grabbed a steak knife. She shoved it into the neck of the man closest to reaching the plate in the order window. Blood sprayed like water from a lawn sprinkler, some of which landed on the plate of stuffed mushrooms.

She had hit his jugular.

The three others who had been fighting with him paused, surprised, looking at the blood that sprayed, then spurted, then fell, then pooled.

The man's body fell. The other three were stricken with shock.

The otherwise nondescript woman with graying hair and a murderous hand used their stunned horror as an opportunity to grab the plate. She ran out, shoving stuffed mushrooms in her mouth even as she went. She seemingly didn't mind that some of them were coated with blood.

The police were called, reports were written. The ambulance had arrived in time to save the man's life.

The culprit was captured within the hour. She had been found crouched beside the dumpster behind the restaurant, licking a silver plate with red etching so hard that her bottom teeth tore into the bottom of her tongue. She must have mistaken her own blood for sauce, because when she was apprehended, she only said a single word, over and again as she lunged desperately for the bloodied plate even after she was handcuffed:

"More!" and then, "More!" and "More! More! More! Mooooooooorrrrrrrrreeee!"

It was an open and shut case; one of aggravated assault at the least, and perhaps manslaughter if the man took a turn for the worse. Still, the questions asked by the police to Chef Hue and the remaining witnesses were arduous, repetitive and time consuming. The only answer any of them could provide… or would provide… was that the lady went insane for no reason at all. The witnesses gave each other furtive glances from time to time, as if it had been agreed upon in some secret, silent pact that none would mention that it was a plate of food they had all been fighting over.

Chef Hue had wondered if this incident would be the end of him as he escorted the police officers and the handful of witnesses out of his establishment hours after the stabbing had occurred.

That had been day twenty, the first of many days that Hubert Jenkins – no longer a true chef were he to be honest with himself – didn't leave the restaurant at all. He slept there, inconsolably concerned about the bad publicity such a violent attack in his establishment would bring him. His sleep had been jet and obsidian once again, though beneath the black was an unease, a potential for ill omens to bubble and boil through the onyx of his newly dreamless sleeps. It felt almost as if his nightmares were being suppressed by a force he could neither see nor describe.

When Hubert awoke on the twenty-first day after the appearance of the pot, he was fully clothed, his uniform heavy with nightmare sweat, despite the fact that he was certain he hadn't had a single dream. It didn't take him long to comport himself and leave the small staff break room he had slept in to make his way hesitantly outside the double doors of the main entrance. It was only ten in the morning, hours before the doors opened for lunch. Hours before the doors opened for the daily special to be first served. What he saw outside of those doors first made him take a step backward, then made him grin.

Dozens of people were lined up outside the front of the establishment, and many dozens more made a crude line that tailed around the north side of the building. He envisioned that line tailing all the way up to Canada.

Not yet, Chef Hue had thought to himself. *But maybe soon.*

The crowd roared in ecstasy as Hubert Jenkins gave them a genial wave. He walked across the brief landing and down the three steps that separated the front doors of his restaurant from the patient patrons, smiling and waving all the while.

Is this what superstardom feels like? Is this what celebrity is?

He grinned all the way to the front of the chalkboard. This wasn't the first time he'd had to read it and write a price upon it in front of an audience, but he'd never had an audience such as this before. As he looked at the board while reflecting upon the events of the previous night, he was surprised to see that, for the first time, the board had repeated an item.

At first, he was terrified that the magic of the thing had vanished, and the board had gone unchanged overnight. His heart vaulted into his throat, and his eyes began to water. Then he noticed there were words written on the board that hadn't been there the previous day. Initially, he had wanted to laugh at the updated message but worried about what was written below the daily special, and if it would be deemed insensitive of him to find humor in it considering the previous night's violence.

He took into account the response from the crowd who had already seen the item written upon the chalkboard. He gauged them, and when he began to write the price of that day's special dish, he noted their collective hush. They were silent until he stepped away, revealing the completed board:

DAILY SPECIAL

BACK BY
POPULAR DEMAND

STUFFED
PORTOBELLO
MUSHROOMS

TO DIE FOR!

$100 PER PLATE

:)

The crowd burst into raucous cheer, as though a hundred dollars for a plate of stuffed mushrooms was reasonable, even generous. The cheers rang madly as Hubert made his way back into the restaurant and to his kitchen. The noise from outside the front doors never diminished during the two hours between his marking the price and the restaurant officially opening for business.

Daily SPECIAL

LASAGNA..**12**

"Would it be okay if I took some of that lasagna home, Chef?" Andrea, one of the newer waitresses, asked after closing one evening. She peered through the order window and into the kitchen at Hue, who had his back to her.

He was preparing to close the pot for the night. He had to fight against reaching both hands in and shoveling the pasta into his mouth. He'd already had four servings that day.

It still astounded Chef Hue at the end of each night, after serving hundreds of people from the pot, that it never once emptied; the quantity never lessened for long. He turned to the order window and looked back at the busty, brown-skinned beauty he had hired three months prior, a month after the cast iron pot had initially changed his life.

He had hired her for the specific purpose of fucking her. Skills and experience were no longer necessary when it came to the waitresses he took under his employ. Hue had eliminated his entire menu. The customers were only interested in the daily special, which was perfectly fine with him. Since the pot had appeared (and perhaps before that, if he were honest with himself), Hue had lost his passion for cooking. With the pot in his kitchen, Hue was well on his way to celebrity status, and that's what he had truly always wanted.

"You know the rule, Andrea," he said, trying to maintain his composure with the lid of the pot still in his hand, the scent and steam from the lovely lasagna rising toward his face, tantalizing and teasing his senses. Closing the lid for the night was always the most difficult thing for the chef to do. He wanted more. He always wanted more. Sometimes, in his weaker moments, he tried to see if he could finish what was in that pot at the end of the night. Though eat as he may, he never could accomplish the task. With great effort, Hue turned to face Andrea.

Despite the delicious food he had access to twenty-four hours of each day, seven days of each week, the chef appeared to be wasting away; he had lost at least fifteen pounds since the kitchen staff had been dismissed. His skin was pallid, his hair thinning.

Andrea, who hadn't seen much of the chef since being hired, gasped at his appearance. Hue smiled. The smile creased his already rapidly aging face, making him look ten years older than the thirty-five he actually was. She had remembered Chef Hue being much younger than he appeared now.

"What's the matter, sweetheart?" the chef asked, as if oblivious to his physical changes. These days, he wasn't as concerned with his appearance as he had once been. These days, he was only concerned with his pot, and the daily special within it. His voice sounded like that of a man who had been chain smoking for half of his life, though Hue had never once touched a cigarette. It wasn't the same voice that Andrea recalled.

"N-nothing, Chef Hue. I was just hoping for something to take home," she said, her voice shaky.

"Don't I pay you enough for you to buy groceries, Andrea? Or am I expected to give you handouts as well?"

"You do, Chef. I just wanted to try the food you cook. The smell is amazing, and I've been hoping to have a bit for a long time now. I just..." She couldn't finish the statement. Her shock from the sight of the chef's physical appearance was wearing off, but her lust for the food in the pot had suddenly become so strong it bordered on sexual. The smell of the lasagna from the still unlidded pot wafted toward her. Her mouth began to water, her stomach tightened, and her underwear rapidly dampened.

"You just...?" the chef asked, knowing exactly what was happening to his newest waitress. He was now using the lid to fan the steam from the pot toward Andrea, who had become obviously agitated. It was a surprise to the chef that she didn't try to leap through the order window and directly into the pot. He briefly thought back to Albert's chewed and bleeding hands, and the woman who had nearly committed murder for a plate of mushrooms.

"I just want it." The words fell rather than projected from her mouth. Speaking was becoming more difficult for Andrea, as was thinking. The smell was blotting out all reason, the steam reaching her synapses and stimulating her in ways she had never known.

"The rule, Andrea, is that no one on the staff gets to eat the food I make. It's for customers only. Do you understand?"

"Yes, Chef."

"If I give you a taste, I'll have to fire you. Are you okay with that?"

"Yes, Chef." No hesitation. No pause for thought of how losing her job might impact her life.

Andrea's underwear was now soaked through.

She vaguely heard the front door behind her being opened, closed, then locked; Brian, one of the bartenders, was gone for the night. It was only Chef Hue and her alone in the empty restaurant... alone with a pot that emanated a smell that was driving her insane.

"Stop staring like a dumb fucking mule. Get in here," Chef Hue demanded. The perverse expression on his face aging him another year or two. Andrea obliged, though walking was pleasantly uncomfortable for her. She felt her moisture dripping down her leg and into her shoes, her thighs rubbing together awkwardly as she tried to maximize the feeling that was emanating from between them. She opened the door to the kitchen, the aroma assailed her once again, even stronger this time, making her knees weak. She took a shaky step toward the pot.

"Stop," Chef Hue stated calmly. Andrea stopped.

"Crawl," he demanded. "Slowly." Andrea dropped to her knees so quickly and with such a crash that Hue thought she may have fractured a kneecap. She seemed indifferent toward any pain she may have felt, her entire focus on the pot full of the delicious smelling lasagna she so badly wanted. The food inspired a craving greater than any she had ever experienced. Crawling was of little consequence to her if it meant she would satisfy that craving.

With her face low to the ground, her pencil skirt rode up her hips, nearly revealing her full, round bottom as it wiggled in the air behind her while she made her way toward the stove. She had nearly reached it when Chef Hue placed his foot on her forehead, stopping her progress. She yelped, more from the frustration of being restrained than for any other reason. It felt as though there was a fire in her stomach. A fire that threatened not only to continuously burn, but to explode.

"Patience, young lady. Appetizer first," the chef said with a maniacal grin on his face as he stood between the young woman and the pot while unzipping the fly of his trousers. Andrea didn't think twice about it. She sat back on her heels, ripped open her shirt. Buttons flew and skittered all over the kitchen floor. She undid her already revealing bra, causing her large breasts to tumble free. She then opened her mouth as wide as she could. Chef Hue laughed hysterically as he pulled out his semi-rigid penis.

A month or so after the pot had appeared in his life, Hubert had begun having trouble gaining and maintaining erections. His mind was so focused on the daily special that he didn't mind this too much; his craving for sexual satisfaction was dwarfed in comparison to his craving for his pot and all its wonders. This, however, was an opportunity he couldn't pass up. He would get a taste of the chocolate he had so desired during his more virile days, and he'd be rid of her soon after. She had already seen too much.

Andrea, the soon to be fired waitress, wrapped her mouth around him. It had always been one of Hubert's favorite feelings, the initial contact of a warm mouth on his skin. Yet, lately, the sensation felt dulled. It had been this way since the night before the pot had appeared, a night that had nearly been blurred out of his memory entirely. He had only been intimate with three or four women in the months since. Which was a dramatic decrease from the usual three or four women he would bed on any given week. Each time was the same: decent or disappointing. Sometimes so disappointing that he often didn't bother to finish, frequently going limp in the middle of these forays.

The usual response was for the chef to dismiss the female, to send her away. He didn't mind. He didn't feel ashamed or embarrassed. He simply went to sleep thinking about what the next day's special would be. Yet, as Chef Hue had his fingers deeply entrenched in Andrea's curly hair, he felt something spectacular that he hadn't for months. He felt an excitement from something other than the pot behind him. Or so he thought. But as he watched her head move back and forth with a speed and vigor he hadn't experienced in all his years, he understood that this too was because of the pot. She was hungry. Not for him, but for what he guarded so closely. And to taste what was in the pot, she would do anything he asked of her. He was going to ask her to turn around. He was going to tell her that he wanted to treat her like a little doggy. He was going to degrade her simply because he could. But her hunger overwhelmed his perversion. She had brought her appetizer to its completion within three minutes of his presenting it to her. He zipped up his pants with barely enough time to stop her from lunging at the pot.

"No, Andrea. I'll serve you. You have to respect my kitchen." He was still throbbing down below from the work she had done on him.

She used the back of her hand to wipe her lips and chin, and, with much restraint, managed to hold her ground. At this point she was visibly shaking. A thin film of sweat had begun to form on her forehead and chest.

"Yes, Chef," she said, with much more patience than she actually felt. Chef Hue reached behind him, into the pot with his bare hand. He ignored the heat that seared his skin, as he had on many occasions prior. He collected a handful of lasagna and, without warning, shoved it into Andrea's mouth. She hadn't been prepared for the offering, causing most of it to fall onto the ground.

Chef Hue watched with muted delight as the young woman with the vacuum for a mouth kneeled and ate the food from the floor like a dog from its bowl. He thought of his mother, dead in a bowl of fried ramen and spam, and he laughed.

Chef Hue very much enjoyed the sight of this young waitress with an ass that wouldn't quit lapping up the lasagna directly from the ground. Her ass would never have to quit, because, as they had discussed, she was officially fired. And, for some odd reason she would never understand, as she licked pasta sauce from between the tiles of the dirty kitchen floor, Andrea was okay with that.

Daily SPECIAL

PORK CHOPS **13**

It continued that way; the way it had been with Andrea and the lasagna. Chef Hue could only become satisfied sexually if the woman he was with was stirred into a frenzied state by the aroma from his pot. He enjoyed the sex, but it wasn't about the physical sensation as it once had been. It was more about the control he had. The control the pot gave him.

The turnover for his wait staff was immense. Chef Hue would fan the fumes, fuck them and then fire them. He didn't think twice about it. With the growing popularity of the restaurant, he had thousands of resumes to choose from at any given time.

The celebrity that Hubert had dreamed of from the moment his mind had been capable of dreaming was now his. It wasn't how he had imagined it, however. What a young, pudgy, awkward Hubert Jenkins had always fantasized of was the jet-setting lifestyle. He imagined flying from city to city, then country to country, all over the globe. He imagined walking down red carpets of award shows and attending Hollywood movie premieres that he would have absolutely zero interest in, just to say that he was important enough to have been there.

What actually occurred was quite different. By the time the first camera found Chef Hue – nearly a month after the pot had appeared – he had moved into his restaurant entirely, not wanting to be away from the pot for any stretch of time. The lease of his condo wouldn't be up for another eight months, but Hue no longer cared about such things as leases. He had money pouring out of every orifice. So much so that he only kept the restaurant open for six hours each day. Between 2 p.m. and 8 p.m. the daily special was served at two hundred dollars a plate. Guests were only allowed to sit for ten minutes at a time.

There wasn't a single complaint.

Hue no longer had to rely on false reviews on the internet to bring customers to his restaurant, the pot's production was all the promo he needed.

Hue was making a killing.

Deep down he knew that he could put whatever price tag he wanted on his daily special and he would still have a full house, but it wasn't about the money. It was all about the pot.

There were times when Hubert would stay in the kitchen all night with the lid of the pot in one hand, waiting for the special to change. Waiting for the pot to do its magic. He stood for six, seven, eight hours at a time, yet never once did he see how the pot worked. If he turned his head, blinked deeply or began to fall asleep in the wee hours of the morning, things inside of the pot would change instantly. From pork chops in mushroom sauce to a pot full of brisket in an instant.

He did the same with the chalkboard outside, waiting, wondering how the letters could get there in his exact writing without him realizing. Neither pot nor chalkboard provided him an answer.

As frustrated as he was each time they would switch without him being aware of how, he was even more amazed.

Amazement and frustration were both trumped by the deep-seated craving that was refreshed every time a new item appeared. On some mornings, Hue would climb onto the stove, crouch down and spend minutes at a time hunched over the pot shoveling handfuls of whatever was inside into his mouth with his bare hands. The media cameras that were outside of the restaurant on a daily basis wouldn't see this, of course. What they would see when they captured a rare image or video of the elusive Chef Hubert Jenkins was a man who seemed haggard and worn down. This didn't surprise his audience in the least. By the time the area outside of Chef Hue's restaurant had become a campground for paparazzi, he was known worldwide as the hardest working chef on the planet. How else could one chef feed hundreds of patrons a day while running a kitchen by himself? Not to mention that the food was – as the chalkboard had once stated – absolutely to die for. Or, perhaps, to kill for.

His first national television interview was with the ladies of the daytime program *Let's Chat*. It was uncomfortable for Chef Hue, simply because he didn't know exactly what to chat about. How could he describe the process of cooking hundreds of plates of food for his customers each day when he had never actually done so? How could he describe his thought process, or the flavor profiles that made each dish so delicious, when, in reality, Hue hadn't even turned on a single burner in months? In the end, he opted to take the mysterious route, wearing sunglasses and a Cincinnati Reds baseball cap with the brim pulled down low on his forehead while talking more about himself than his process. Describing the food, but never how it was made. The nation ate it up – both his air of mystery and the food that came from his kitchen.

Chef Hue would go on to be the headline guest of every talk show on all of the major networks in the developed world for many months. All via satellite, of course. The chef no longer left his restaurant for any reason. To everyone who hadn't been given an opportunity to peek through the order window and see him in the kitchen, Chef Hubert Jenkins had become the lovable, far-too-busy-to-leave-his-kitchen, mysterious, slightly strange, but phenomenal recluse.

He didn't need to go shopping for food because the pot provided more than enough. There was a bathroom and televisions in the restaurant, though Hue had become less and less interested in either of the above as time passed. He rarely drank fluids, and found he was only urinating once every few days. When he did urinate, he would produce streams of piss so dark they were nearly mud brown. And, despite how much he ate from the pot, he could only defecate once every couple of weeks, evacuating loose, syrupy reddish-black feces.

He didn't think much of any of this. His infrequent bathroom visits simply meant more time to spend with his pot. On the days when he would have to do an interview, or make an appearance at the front of the restaurant, or perhaps when he got the rare urge to fuck and fire another waitress (he had lost count of how many he'd let go into before letting go of), he would take a whore's bath using the industrial sink of his kitchen; washing his face and the parts of his body that mattered.

Three months after he had spoken to the ladies of *Let's Chat,* Chef Hue no longer had to worry about washing his hair. Because it, along with some of his teeth, had fallen out. It was at that point that he began to decline the media scrums, the requests for personal statements, even the satellite interviews.

The allure of celebrity no longer appealed to Hubert Jenkins.

Daily SPECIAL

CROW'S FEET..**14**

Fifteen months after the cast iron pot had begun to burn atop his otherwise lifeless stove, Hue had lost seventy pounds, an entire head of hair, many of his teeth, and the majority of his mind. His thirty-six-year-old body looked as though it had aged thirty years more. Crow's feet clawed at what was once a smooth face. Liver spots and varicose veins began to make appearances all over his yellowish skin. His penis, which had once made appearances to several women on a regular basis, was now completely (and seemingly permanently) flaccid. Not even the hypersexual mindset the pot induced when a woman was near did anything for him these days. Yet the loss of his libido bothered him as little as the loss of his hair, or the aging of his body.

So long as the pot continued to cook, Hue was content.

Unbeknownst to Hue, however, there was a growing discontent among some of his former staff members who had been so unfairly and unceremoniously relieved of their duties. Albert the cook had never gotten over the way he had been let go, the way he'd demeaned himself by crawling on the floor to taste the food that Chef Hue was claiming as his own. When he was able to briefly let go of that terrible memory, he only had to look at the scars on his hands to be reminded again. He was also reminded by the fact that he was broke, unemployed, had moved back in with his mother. In the basement again. And it wasn't fair.

None of it was fucking fair.

Albert had seen the pot first. Albert had tasted from it before Chef Hue had even known of its existence. But it was Albert who got nothing while Chef Hue got everything. The money. The women. The fame. Albert hadn't allowed himself to get over this injustice. More importantly, Albert hadn't gotten over the allure of the pot. The scent, the flavor, the feeling that had come from the pot was enough to drive a man to madness. And, judging from the interviews he had seen on television, the chef was slowly arriving at that destination.

Albert watched and waited for an opportunity to get back at the chef, to expose him for the lunatic fraud he truly was. For months he sat in his vehicle, parked in the shadows of the lower level of the two-story parking lot across the street from *A Lovely Hue Restaurant and Bar*. From there, he kept an eye on the restaurant, observing the ever-extending lineups.

With each passing day the queue grew longer and longer until it nearly wrapped around the entire neighborhood. On many of those days, Albert had to fight himself not to join the lineup. He wanted whatever was in that pot so badly. Everything he had eaten ever since the bisque and the macaroni and cheese tasted like newspaper to him. His lack of desire for all food that didn't come from the cast iron pot had helped him lose the weight he had wanted to lose since he was a teenager. Fifty-six pounds and counting. He would have been happy about that at any other point in his life. But now, at this time, Albert knew there could be no happiness without access to the pot. And all that stood between Albert and the access he needed was one man.

Albert had witnessed the magic of the pot himself, and he vowed on his life that he would see it again. One taste was not enough. Not nearly. Not when the pot called out to him in his sleep – the little sleep he got these days.

Albert had been there watching when the black waitress with the thick curls came running out of the restaurant late one night, looking frazzled and confused, her shirt wide open and her breasts barely contained within her bra. He didn't know her, but he recognized that she was one of the waitresses by her attire – a pale blue blouse and a black pencil skirt.

He considered chasing her to ask what had happened inside, but decided to let her go her own way. She may have been a damsel in distress, but he was far from a knight in shining armor. Though when he saw Brenda, a waitress he did know, leave the restaurant in similar fashion a month later, followed by Janice some weeks after that, then Jessica and then Shelby (who had emerged from the restaurant completely nude), as well as a few others that Albert figured had come after his time there, he understood that something was seriously wrong. And, if he didn't do anything about it, then the something that was wrong would only get worse.

Eventually, one of the young women wouldn't make it out at all, and the guilt of his inaction would leave him with as much blood on his hands as the chef's were sure to have. He looked down at those scarred hands. Hands that he had nearly chewed through because they had been soaking in the flavor of the pot, flavor that he longed for even as he stared at the fallout of such a powerful desire. Just what was Chef Hue making these women do to get a taste of what he had? He knew the answer to that question, and it made him shudder. He shuddered, not only out of sympathy for the girls, but because he had begun to seriously contemplate just what he would be willing to do to have access to that pot again. It was a question he often asked himself, and the answer terrified him to no end.

He would do anything.

Anything.

Once Albert had caught wind of the chef's newfound superstardom, he understood that he had to have the pot for himself at all costs. It would be Albert being interviewed. It would be Albert making all the money he wanted. It would be Albert who would get the respect that he had never been given while working under Chef Hue. They both knew that Albert was the better and more devoted cook. They both knew that Albert had been the one to discover the pot in the first place; to taste its wonders before anyone else. Finders keepers, losers weepers.

The pot was rightfully his.

And it wasn't just the pot. Everything the chef now had should have been Albert's: the fanfare, the interviews, even the waitresses (and a few of the barmen, if Albert was truly honest with himself). Yet he had nothing. Nothing except for a beat-up Volvo, a smart phone, and a pair of binoculars.

Yes, Albert thought to himself, *I'm entitled to so much more.*

He licked his lips in anticipation. He could almost smell the pot from the parking lot across the street from the restaurant. It was his.

And it was calling him.

Daily SPECIAL

A DISH BEST SERVED COLD............................**15**

It was when Albert noticed two things that he finally devised his plan. The first thing Albert noticed was that the waitresses who usually stormed out after business hours never returned. The second thing Albert noticed was that Hubert stopped leaving the restaurant entirely. Albert knew the chef had been living in *A Lovely Hue* for over a year at that point, but during that time he had come out to do the occasional press report or interview, had come out to update the price on the chalkboard each morning, had come out to wave to his adoring customers. Then all of that stopped. It took Albert eight days of continuous surveillance before he was convinced that Chef Hue was never going to leave the restaurant again.

    The only reason Albert was certain that Chef Hue hadn't died was because business continued to go on as usual. The chef was now closer to the pot than he had ever been, giving little opportunity for Albert to take what he believed to be his property. He had to act fast.

    The plan Albert came up with wasn't much of a plan at all. Much like any fiend under the spell of a drug, Albert didn't really think about things in the long term. What he did think of was gathering the women who had been fired, ambushing Chef Hue as he slept in the restaurant, and stealing the pot. Albert still had the key, and he hoped the chef had been too concerned with his pot to replace the locks. But even if he had changed the locks, they could break a window and climb into the restaurant.

That was the plan. And it was the only thing Albert had been able to cook up since leaving the restaurant. The job he had once loved was now meaningless to him. He could never cook anything as delicious as what he had tasted from the pot, so what was the point of cooking at all? Because Chef Hue had stolen the pot and the only job he had ever loved from him, what Albert now prepared was revenge, a dish best served cold.

He was content with the plan, spartan as it was. Gathering a posse would be the most difficult aspect. Fortunately, Albert had developed a friendship with one of the bartenders at *A Lovely Hue* before he'd been fired. The friendship had been an unusually strong one for two males who had only recently met. Shame, along with his obsessive stalking of Chef Hue, had prevented Al from keeping in touch with the barman since he had been fired. He hoped Brian still cared enough to help him. Brian was the only person Albert could think of reaching out to once he decided that his plan had to be put into action.

From his car, late one night while watching the restaurant, he made the call.

"Hello?" Brian answered his phone groggily. Albert could hear the shifting and rustling of bedsheets through the line.

"Brian. It's me. Albert." It was three in the morning when Albert had worked up the courage to make the call to the friend who he cared about deeply, but who also made him feel a tad uncomfortable for reasons Albert couldn't, or wouldn't, admit to himself.

"Ally? Oh my God! I've called you a hundred times since I heard you got fired. No one knows what happened to you and the staff. It's been SO crazy at Hue's!"

Albert cringed at being called Ally, and at the restaurant being referred to as Hue's. Albert knew Hue was the owner, but it had been Albert cooking and taking care of the kitchen staff while Hue was daydreaming of celebrity chef fame and screwing whichever waitress would open her legs for him. It was Albert who had discovered the pot that had changed everything! The pot was his! That kitchen was his! The credit belonged to him! He struggled to stop himself from spilling all of this to Brian. He took a deep breath to regain his composure.

"You know I hate it when you call me Ally, Brian... I've been okay. I wanna know about the waitresses Hue's fired since I've been gone."

"Oh my God!" Brian yelled into his device. Albert had to hold the phone away from his ear. "I couldn't even tell you what's going on there, All...bert! The place is so packed. Waitresses come and go. We don't ask about it because no one wants to be the next to go. It's good money, Albert. *Really* good. I'm sorry you and the others didn't get a chance to see it."

Albert didn't have to see it to know what it must have looked like. He thought about the long lineups, knowing what people would be willing to pay for the contents of the pot.

"That's alright, Brian. Thanks for saying so. But what I need right now are the names and numbers of a few of the waitresses that've been canned since I was given the boot. It sounds sappy, but I wanna start a kind of support group. No one should be treated the way I was, and I'm sure I'm not the only one who feels this way."

There was a pause on the other end as Brian considered this. Always empathetic, the barman began to scroll through his phone. Albert heard the clicking and sliding of the mobile device from Brian's end and smiled. It was good to know that not everyone had been corrupted by Chef Hue.

A few moments, as well as an awkward, choked up goodbye later, and Albert had what he wanted: the names and phone numbers of several of the waitresses who had been fired since the chef had dismissed him from his own kitchen.

Daily SPECIAL

TAMALES..16

Of the seven waitresses Albert attempted to contact, two would not answer his calls or respond to his messages. One phone number was out of service. And one phone call was answered by a distraught woman who disclosed tearfully that her daughter had killed herself shortly after being fired from the restaurant. Her daughter hadn't been able to stop raving about tamales before she had ended her life. The woman told Albert that she never wanted to hear anything about Chef Hue or his restaurant ever again before hanging up abruptly.

The news of the suicide shook Albert. Not only because he wondered if that young lady's blood was on his hands since he hadn't done anything to stop Chef Hue sooner, but because he understood why she had killed herself. There had been several sleepless nights Albert had spent thinking about the pot, about the bisque, the macaroni and cheese. The idea of never tasting anything that splendid again had caused him to contemplate ending it all.

He steeled himself, focused on his flimsy plan, and continued to reach out to the other waitresses he had seen sprinting from the restaurant dismayed, disoriented, and disheveled. He couldn't help the girl who had taken her life, but he could take down Chef Hue for her sake. And for the sake of the pot.

Three of the young women he reached out to agreed to meet with him. All three of them agreed, without very much enticement, to go forward with his plan of breaking and entering, though none of them for a moment considered this to be a crime. Much like Albert, the waitresses had become obsessed with what they had tasted from the pot. They would have done just about anything he asked if it meant they would get to eat from it again.

The former cook sat in his car watching the restaurant, smiling each time he received one of their enthusiastic acceptances of his flimsy plan. He wondered if this was how the chef felt when he bent these women to his every whim. The thought made his smile broaden as he dreamed of all he could accomplish, all he could have when the pot would once again belong to him.

His smile was bittersweet, however. He understood, just by listening to the desperation in the voices of the waitresses when they spoke about the pot and its delicacies, that they were willing to kill for the pot. Willing to kill the chef and probably kill Albert and each other along with him. But he was okay with them trying.

Albert had always been very skillful with a knife.

Daily SPECIAL

CHEESECAKE **17**

Andrea was one of the three waitresses who agreed to help Albert with his endeavor. She was the most enthusiastic about the plan. Her resentment was apparent when she and Albert met to discuss the details at a community park not far from *A Lovely Hue*. She didn't resent Chef Hue because he had made her crawl on the floor, it wasn't because he had coerced her into performing fellatio upon him. She resented the chef because he had only given her a handful of the lasagna she had so desperately desired. Albert had explained to her that the pot could have supplied her with enough lasagna to last a lifetime, and that was all it took to stir her into a frenzy.

The stories of the others were similar to that of Andrea's. Albert would learn of their experiences upon meeting each waitress.

It was Jasmine who Albert saw next. She had insisted they meet late at night in a place with few people around, eventually agreeing to rendezvous at a twenty-four-hour coffee shop. Not long after sitting across from Albert, she had removed the scarf and oversized sunglasses that covered most of her face, and he understood why she hadn't wanted to be seen. Albert looked at a network of long and loud pink marks that marred an otherwise pretty face. Jasmine had yet to heal from her encounter with Chef Hue.

She told Albert that the chef had roughly shoved his semi-stiff pecker into her ass, promising to give her a portion of cheesecake that had been made within the pot when he was done. Once finished with the short-haired brunette, he took a portion of cake from the pot and smashed it in her face like a child would to a birthday party clown. He had laughed while she licked portions of the crumbled cheesecake from the floor and her hands before wiping it from her face and stuffing the cake into her mouth in a state of hysteria. She had cut her face with her fingernails in her rush to get every last morsel. Then Jasmine had bit into her fingers as she tried to take in the immense flavor that still lingered on her hands. It was as though her face had wanted revenge for the damage her hands had done to it. Albert could relate. He looked down at his own scarred hands.

Jasmine had been a bloody mess by the time she left the restaurant that night. Later, she told her family and friends she had been attacked by a feral cat that had jumped out of the trees and onto her head. She had been so distraught and discombobulated that no one had doubted her story.

The third of the waitresses was Shelby, with her pink-blond hair, pouty mouth, and bright green eyes. She had paid zero attention to the once-portly cook when the two had worked together. Albert knew that he would have her full attention once the pot was his again. He tried to dismiss his dirty thoughts as he heard her story.

Albert felt ashamed as he fought to contain his arousal while sitting across from Shelby in her apartment. As Shelby told her tale, she lifted her shirt to show him the angry red splotches and raised skin that littered her stomach and breasts.

The chef had burned her.

When Shelby had requested to try some of the beef stew she had been serving during what turned out to be her final shift, Chef Hue had asked her to lay on her back on the kitchen floor. He seemed to have no interest in touching her, only watching her while giving her instructions, commanding her to take off her clothes and work herself until she came.

When she started to play with herself, the contents of the pot had begun to boil intensely. The sound of the bubbling stew seemed to sooth Shelby. Seemed to make her believe that listening to Chef Hue was the right thing to do. She continued to masturbate aggressively on the cold, dirty floor as the chef grabbed his soup ladle. He poured ladle after ladle of boiling liquid onto the young lady's naked torso until she was seized by her orgasm.

The entire time she played with herself, she licked and pawed at the hot stew that was being poured on her body. She didn't understand that she had been severely burned until she had walked nearly five miles toward her apartment, still naked, still licking at herself periodically to see if she could taste the stew that had been poured on her. A neighbor had called the police upon spotting her. When the officers caught up to the naked woman walking in a haze down the street, they noticed the large patches of red, peeling skin all over her. She was too ashamed and confused to admit what had happened, so she simply said she didn't remember. Shelby had been undergoing intensive psychotherapy ever since.

Of the three women he was able to convince to join his cause, Shelby was the only one he had met previously, and the waitresses hadn't worked together for long before their firings. The quartet were essentially strangers to each other, though their collective purpose made them feel close as kin.

Less than a week after Brian had given Albert the waitresses' contact information, the former cook and the three young women walked toward the rear of *A Lovely Hue Restaurant and Bar* ready to put their plan into action.

Daily SPECIAL

A BUFFET OF FLESH...............................18

Albert had met with each of the waitresses one-on-one prior to this day, but seeing them all standing there as a group made it all real. He looked at each of them as they stood by the restaurant's back door and was taken aback by how outlandishly gorgeous they were. Albert had never been in such intimate proximity to so many beautiful women at once. Again, the envy and hatred he felt for Chef Hue spiked in his chest, solidifying his purpose, dispersing any residual doubt about his plan.

Once the pot was his, he would not only have access to the most amazing meals one could dream of each day, he would also have a buffet of flesh at all times, women just like these to choose from any time he wanted them. He gave each waitress a longing lecherous look, which they interpreted as last-minute doubt.

"Are you okay? You're not having second thoughts, are you?" Shelby asked. Albert gave her a wan smile.

If you only knew the thoughts I was having, he thought to himself.

"No. No second thoughts. I'm just excited is all." *For a lot of reasons.*

He allowed his mind to drift, not only to what he would do for the pot, but what he could get others to do for him once the pot was in his possession. His excitement grew. He thought of the last televised interview he had seen of Chef Hue. The man seemed to have lost dozens of pounds. He had appeared frail beyond his years. Albert didn't think it would take much effort to strongarm Hue and take the pot. And if they were caught? What would the chef tell the police? Would he say that he had fired his employees unjustly, and now they were disgruntled and had come back to steal his magic pot? Probably not. If things went askew, Albert would explain to the officers that the employees were simply there to discuss severance owed by the chef to those he terminated without cause. Why were they there to discuss such a matter at two o'clock in the morning? Because they wanted to avoid the throng of reporters that always swarmed around the restaurant until the late hours of night. They knew the chef stayed in his kitchen at all hours.

All of this played in Albert's head as he approached the back door. The door that led to the kitchen. The door he hoped his key would still unlock. The four of them tingled and tremored with the nervous anticipation of junkies about to get their long-awaited fix. There was never a single word of protest or question about the plan. To each of them, it was simply something that had to be done.

They had all fantasized about what delicacies the pot would hold for them. Albert yearned for the mac and cheese he had never gotten enough of. For Andrea, it was the lasagna she had only had a chance to sample rather than to feast upon. Cheesecake for Jasmine. For Shelby, it was a proper chance to have the beef stew in her stomach rather than on her belly.

Their hunger increased with each step toward the door.

Albert removed the rope which held the key from around his neck. He exhaled slowly, praying that they wouldn't have to physically break into the place. When the key slid smoothly into the keyhole, Albert grinned. He twisted the key and heard the tumblers roll and click loudly. The door was unlocked; Albert was very pleased. Pleased but not surprised. The chef had likely been too consumed by the pot to remember Albert's duplicate key.

Albert gave a look of encouragement to his small group of bandits. Jasmine giggled excitedly. Andrea admonished her with a frown, placing her index finger to her lips. They waited nervously for Albert to open the door, not knowing quite what to expect, but each with eager anticipation of what they hoped they would discover.

Albert opened the door.

Three loud beeps blared throughout the restaurant.

The four bandits paused.

"Fuck," Albert whispered, understanding that the beeping noise was a warning, an indicator that an alarm was about to go off. There hadn't been an alarm when he had worked there.

Albert looked around desperately, searching for a pad or device that might deactivate the system. The others remained silent. They shook from nervousness and trepidation. Still, desire for the pot triumphed over any fear that might have caused them to abandon their plan.

Albert began to run. Not back in the direction they had come from; instead, he ran in the direction of the kitchen where he hoped he could grab the pot and make a quick escape with it before the alarm went off and the police arrived in response to it.

He had nearly made it halfway there when the lights in the kitchen turned on, causing him to stop abruptly.

Standing in the entryway to the kitchen, between Albert and the pot, was Hubert Jenkins.

Daily SPECIAL

TOMATO SOUP **19**

Albert gasped upon seeing Chef Hue. The man he had once worked beneath was now nearly unrecognizable. His skin wrapped his bones as though all of the meat that had once made him up was gone. Liver spots dotted a bald head which had held a full, lush head of hair only a year before; wrinkles lined his face, crisscrossing over once-handsome features. Hue's posture was stooped and his frame decrepit. He looked as though he had shrunk by half a foot. If not for the familiar green eyes and the chef's sharp facial features, Albert would have sworn he was looking at someone's great-grandfather.

"Chef?" Albert asked incredulously.

"Al," Chef Hue responded, sounding unsurprised. His voice was raspy and strained, like a man long deprived of water. "Good to see you again." The chef smiled, revealing a toothless mouth. Albert cringed. He heard the women behind him gasp. One of them screamed, the sound muffled by the hands covering the mouth which had created it. Chef Hue reached both hands into the pockets of the baby blue bathrobe he wore. He withdrew his left hand, revealing a small device that resembled a remote control, and then his right hand, which gripped a pistol.

On the small remote control, Hue clicked several buttons. Five more beeps sounded off through the building, indicating that the alarm had been disarmed. Placing the remote back in his pocket, Hue shakily pointed the pistol at Albert. Behind the chef, Albert could see the lidless pot. He could hear it as it began to boil. He saw the steam begin to rise from it. His mouth watered in anticipation. Albert barely noticed the death device pointed at his face, nor did the three women pay it heed as they sprang toward the source of the heavenly scent the moment it entered their nostrils. Shocked, Hue turned his attention and pistol to his former waitresses who were rushing past Albert, toward the pot.

The gun went off.

Shelby hit the floor with a bullet in her hip. The kickback of the gun was too powerful for the decrepit chef. He lost his balance, teetering, threatening to topple backward. Seeing his chance, Albert rushed at Hue, ramming the chef with his shoulder and knocking him over, which wasn't a difficult thing to do.

Hue's rapidly aging body hit the ground with a soft thud, and slid, feather-light, across the floor, stalling in the middle of the large kitchen area. The gun flew from his grip and fired again as it clanked violently against the ground, skipping and skidding across the floor away from where Hubert had slid, coming to a stop beneath the sink on the far side of the kitchen. Albert and the others checked themselves briefly to see if the second bullet had hit them. They were unscathed.

"The pot!" each person in the room exclaimed at once. It was right there for the taking. The fumes floated seductively toward them. Tomato soup! Albert, Andrea, and Jasmine were close enough to see the orange-red substance bubbling within the pot. Shelby wept on the floor, but she never stopped slithering toward the pot, slowly smearing a trail of blood against the filthy kitchen tiles.

Chef Hue, meanwhile, sat up with great effort, trying to gather his strength. The chef slowly got to his feet as Albert and two of his former waitresses (whose names escaped him) all put their hands on the pot at the same time. He smiled to himself, knowing that after several thousand attempts of his own to move the pot, it wouldn't budge. His toothless leer grew larger as he relished in the knowledge that their hands were burning as they touched the brewing pot. Yet they wouldn't let go, each hopeful to carry the pot off and feed from it forever.

Chef Hue nearly began to gloat aloud until he saw something that made his smile vanish entirely.

The pot had shifted toward Albert.

Hue's guts jumped to his throat, but not high enough to stop his cry of protest. What Hue had intended to be a fierce shout came out as barely a whimper. It was the feeble, trembling voice of an old man that passed from between Hue's thin, dry lips. Hubert still hadn't become accustomed to it. Nor was he accustomed to the weak legs beneath him. He wobbled toward the bandits, then used those shaky legs to lunge forward with all of his will and all the strength he could muster.

The chef mistimed his jump (or had assumed he could still jump as far as he'd once been able to). Albert easily sidestepped the frail man and watched Hue hit his head and shoulder on the front of the oven, crumpling to its base, dazed but not out. He had just managed to grasp the edge of the still bubbling pot. No, not *the* pot. *His* pot. In Hubert's mind it could never belong to anyone else. The pot must have agreed with him because, as he looked up to see if he had successfully managed to pull it toward him, it nodded.

After over a year of trying, it had finally moved for him. He knew, at that moment, the pot *was* truly his. Hubert Jenkins laughed even as the little cauldron spilled over.

He continued to laugh as the tomato soup cascaded down upon him, scalding the thin skin that wrapped his bones, cooking it through. The feeling swelling through his body at that moment was one of exquisite agony. Mindless of the pain, he cackled with sheer joy as he opened his mouth to welcome the sweet and spicy searingly hot wonderment down his throat. Soup was one of the few things he could consume since he had lost the last of his teeth a month or so prior.

As the seemingly endless fall of tomato soup showered over him (his mouth wide open to accept as much as he could catch), Hue thought of nothing but the relief of being able to enjoy the dish as it was supposed to be enjoyed, rather than having to gum or crush or mash his meals in order to devour them, as he had recently been forced to do. For this, Hubert was grateful.

Even though he was being melted alive, Hubert felt nothing but bliss.

Albert wasn't happy, however. He tried to right the pot, tried to set it straight so as not to waste its precious contents, but to no avail. He and the three ladies could do nothing but watch as the pot poured an inexplicable amount of soup onto the chef. The smell in the air changed as the chef's boiling skin and the little bit of flesh he had left were added to the fragrance of the tomato soup. To Albert's dismay, the pot was emptying. It wasn't forever full as he had recalled.

He did everything in his power to right the pot before it was completely devoid of the soup that had called to them. He and the waitresses tried unsuccessfully to shovel the soup back into the pot with their palms. Changing tact, Albert burned the lower half of his face as he stooped down and caught some of the cascading flow of orange-red liquid with his mouth as it fell.

Once again, it seemed that he would have to come to terms with the fact that the contents of the pot were reserved for Chef Hue.

Lucky bastard, Albert thought as he watched the decrepit Hue, smiling as he was saturated in the burning hot tomato soup. The pot emptied entirely once Hue was completely covered from head to toe. The soup was so rich and thick that it clung to the former chef like a paste. Hue twitched beneath the layer of steaming hot liquid, his face enveloped entirely, but his grin still grew.

With the pot finally empty, Albert was able to set it correctly on the burner it had once been affixed to. He noted with grim wonder that the six ravens which had once been etched into the side of the pot were now gone. Deep inside of him he understood that the glamor of the pot was lost. Hue had tipped it over and spilled the magic out along with the soup that now smothered him. Albert began to cry. The two women on either side of him did likewise. It was only Shelby, still shuffling on the floor, who decided to seize the opportunity while her fellow bandits mourned.

The soup was still there.

She could still enjoy the soup.

She crawled to the chef, who was now incapacitated, and began to lick the soup from his body.

"Hey!" Andrea and Jasmine yelled simultaneously, angrily. They dropped to the floor and began to lick at Hue's tomato soup-stained robe. Albert joined them after a second's hesitation, on his knees, doing everything he could to get at what he understood would be the last item the pot would ever create.

They kneeled there for several minutes, ignoring Chef Hue's whimpers, trying to get every last drop of the tomato soup.

It was Andrea who noticed first.

Noticed that the orange-red of the soup had turned to a deeper red.

Still, she continued, the flavor was too great for her to stop. Too great for any of them to even question what was happening beneath them. Not until they had satisfied their hunger. Not until every last drop of the soup was gone.

When the soup was gone, when they lifted their faces and looked down, what they saw was Chef Hue. More accurately, his skeleton and tendons, and the torn and shredded bags that had once housed his organs.

Albert recoiled in horror as Shelby snaked backward away from the body. Jasmine and Andrea knelt as if in prayer and held each other tightly.

They all looked from the corpse they had been feasting upon to the pot on the stove. Not only was the pot empty, but it was also completely clean, as though nothing had ever been cooked within it at all. They each began to cry. Sobs and gasps and wheezes rang out through the room.

Emptiness was everywhere.

Meaning had moved on.

They mourned deeply, regrettably, with the understanding that they would never experience a meal as wonderful as the one they'd just had.

∞

In the cool, empty darkness outside, at the front of the restaurant, stood the old-fashioned chalkboard upon its wooden easel. The writing on it had changed from the previous day. It was still the chef's printing, as it had always been, though the police who eventually arrived at the scene and found Hubert's cannibalized corpse would later believe the message upon the board to be a cruel joke played by the perpetrators of the hideous crime.

The chalkboard read:

DAILY SPECIAL

HUBERT JENKINS

LIMITED PORTIONS

☺

THANKS FOR READING!

Daily Special was one of the first stories I ever wrote. Back when I was just writing without any real aim or purpose. I got a cool idea or went through some sort of difficult situation and wrote a story about it. And then that story sat for years. That was the case with *Daily Special* and most of the tales that made up the collection, *How To Make A Monster: The Loveliest Shade of Red*, where *Daily Special* was originally published.

Daily Special was one of the few stories in the collection that was not rooted in my distress. To me, it has always been the bright spot in the gloom of that collection. A collection that many people find too dark to complete, making it so *Daily Special*, the fifth story in the book, has often gone unread. And that's one of the reasons I decided to publish it as an individual novella. The other reason is that this story connects to several of my books, and the overarching world I'm building.

I was nervous going back and rereading *Daily Special*, which I hadn't read since publishing *How To Make A Monster* in 2019. Even though I enjoyed *Daily Special* just as much four years later, I now recognize that if I had this idea now, it would be a very different story. I likely would have made it a novel, elaborated on Chef Hue's backstory, same with Al. I may have even included each perspective of the waitresses. Even as I reread it, I considered rewriting the story and making it fuller. But that would undermine what I meant this story to be when I wrote it back in 2016. I wanted it to be the short, fun, sprint to a gory finish line that I hope you found it to be. So, other than a few minor tweaks, and the improved art and format of the story, this is essentially the same tale you'll find in *How To Make A Monster*.

I first thought of *Daily Special* when the person I was involved with at the time was in my kitchen wanting to cook something. She reached into my cabinet and pulled out a pot. It was an old, yellow, hideous looking thing that I had never in my life seen (and I cooked all the time). I was so jarred by the sight of this unfamiliar piece of cookery that I immediately thought: haunted pot. And not long after, I wrote *Daily Special*.

Realistically, it was probably just a pot I had grabbed from my mom's kitchen at some point, shoved in the corner of my cabinet and forgot all about. But I'm going to stick to the story of a phantom pot showing up in my apartment and allowing me to cook up this story, which may still be my favourite of all my stories. It makes my inner fat kid happy.

I hope you enjoyed it, but, even if you didn't, feel free to leave a review on Goodreads, Amazon, or wherever you talk about books, and let other readers know why. All reviews are appreciated.

I'd like to acknowledge the Food Network for influencing this story. If I hadn't become obsessed with the Food Network while, oddly enough, losing a bunch of weight (sixty pounds, most of which I've managed to keep off!), I would never have had the ingredients necessary to write *Daily Special*. And I wouldn't be able to make a jambalaya that will knock your socks off.

I'd also like to acknowledge Courtney, Rosco, and Ally, who have helped me with nearly all of my books. And, of course, my brother Fred.

Thanks again for reading! And now to get something to eat.

Dimaro

August 29, 2023

THE RED LADY WILL RETURN

If you enjoyed Daily Special and would like to read more about The Red Lady, check out *How To Make A Monster: The Loveliest Shade of Red*, where Daily Special was originally published. *How To Make A Monster* contains 4 novellas, 3 novelettes, and 1 short story.

How To Make A Monster

The Loveliest Shade of Red

FELIX I.D. DIMARO

A man finds himself in a jail cell with no memory of how he got there and no one to let him out, a drug addicted stripper has an accident at work and must face her past demons head on, a young woman searches for answers after waking up in an empty hospital and an empty, darkened, dust-covered world...

How To Make A Monster explores the thin line between humanity and monstrosity which exists inside us all. Containing eight stories, this collection details how one wrong turn, one ill-timed hello, a goodbye that was planned too late, how any step we take can lead us down the path to monstrosity.

ALSO BY FELIX I.D. DIMARO

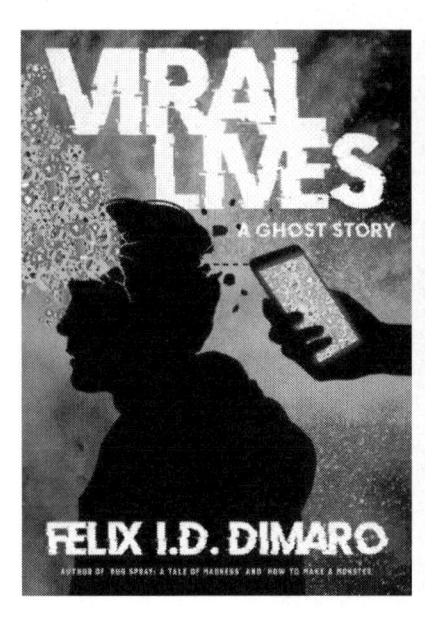

Viral Lives: A Ghost Story: Simon Hinch is a Gore Reporter. He spends late nights in bad places hoping to record violence for a fee. When Simon stumbles upon a man, bloody and dying in the street, he decides to film him instead of help. His footage is a viral sensation, and life is good for Simon. But it turns out that he may not have only captured a man's death on his phone, he may have captured a dead man's soul.

Humane Sacrifice: Losing a pet is never easy. For Melvin Cockburn – fortyish, alone, living in his mother's basement – losing his cat, Lucy, means losing his only friend.
When Lucy is diagnosed with cancer and given no chance to survive, Melvin is desperate for a solution that might save her. When all seems lost, he is approached by a peculiar stranger. Someone who claims to have an alternative method of treatment for his poor, dying cat. What Lucy needs to survive on is life. What she hungers for is a sacrifice or few. And all Melvin has to do to save his cat is provide her with a feast of human souls.

COMING SOON

Everywhere, individuals are waking up in silent cities, darkened places. They are waking up alone, their families and friends gone, their towns empty, most of the planet's population vanished all at once. Electrical grids have stopped functioning, phones and all modes of communication no longer work, vehicles have been permanently stalled. And all that remains, everything that has been left behind, is covered in dust.

The Day of The Dust follows survivors of this sudden apocalypse as they navigate this nearly empty, strange, dusty, lawless world. It will be serialized online for free on Substack at thingsthatkeepmeupatnight.substack.com starting early in 2024. Subscribe to the above Substack for updates, and follow Dimaro on Instagram @thingsthatkeepmeupatnight, or at www.thingsthatkeepmeupatnight.com

Manufactured by Amazon.ca
Bolton, ON